RENE BARJAVEL, THE AUTHOR OF
FUTURE TIMES THREE . . .

"is well known as a journalist and pioneer in
science-fiction. (He has received) the French book-
sellers' prize . . . which has become an important
literary event . . ."

—*The New York Times*

When a pair of scientists choose to plunge
into the unknown and travel back and forth
through the barriers of time, they become
victims of a horrible, mind-twisting trap!

Don't miss this incredible adventure beyond
the realm of reason. It is science-fiction suspense of the highest caliber!

FUTURE TIMES THREE!

FUTURE
TIMES
THREE

Rene Barjavel

Translated by
Margaret Sansone Scouten

AWARD BOOKS
NEW YORK   TANDEM BOOKS
LONDON

CONTENTS

Part I

APPRENTICESHIP

1

1942. It was bitter cold. At dawn Sergeant Mosler discovered the body of a soldier sprawled across the camp latrine, covered with snow. He had frozen to death. His thighs clattered like hollow boards when you rapped them. Four men carried him off. The one who held the head accidentally snapped off his ears.

The Pyrenean hunters of the 27th Battalion, encamped on the border of a beet field, had occupied the village of Vanesse for two months. Today they were to leave for an unknown destination. Peter St. Menoux, the corporal of the squadron, slept uneasily, buried in the straw of the stable. He was tormented by the worries of his seventh tour and the responsibility for seventeen artillerymen, their horses and their gun-wagons. As a civilian he had been a mathematics teacher at Philip-August High School.

His greatest worry was the kitchens. The cooks were always late. Finally, shaking off the straw, he set out toward the field kitchen. He shivered, trying to shorten his large lanky body so as to offer less surface to the cold. Hands thrust into the pockets of his overcoat, back hunched, beret pulled down over his eyes, he ran stiff-legged like a heron across the farm.

"Are you thinking about getting ready? I would prefer not getting bawled out for you again!" he yelled.

Greasy, dirty Corporal Credent slapped him on the shoulder. "Don't worry, old man. It'll come. Peace will come someday. The rear battalion has already arrived." He grinned,

9

showing green teeth. "Do you want something to eat?" Spearing a steak cooking in the flames, he gnawed at the charred meat. From his smoking tin cup, balanced on the log where he sat, rose the mingled odors of coffee and wine.

St. Menoux felt his stomach revolt. "How can you drink that garbage? It smells like a wino's vomit."

Some crows swooped down from the low-hanging clouds and perched in black clusters on an elm standing solitary and forlorn in the middle of the field. It was the only tree left standing after the earlier war. A flurry of snow began to obscure the horizon around the farm, muffling the scattered sounds which rose from the village—the cry of impatient men abusing their animals, the shouts of noncommissioned officers bawling out the men.

Under the sheds the cooks began to load their only cart, a grating, swaying, two-wheeled covered wagon.

"That thing was around for the War of 1914—maybe even the one in 1870," complained Credent. He walked over to help his men pile on sacks of coffee, sugar, rice, potatoes, split peas, beans, lentils, lard, the barrel of frozen wine, the cask of rum, two sides of beef, cases of canned food and crackers, the 120 loaves of bread, the two bundles of hay, the faggots of wood, a half-tub of mustard, the salt, onions, one hundred pounds of carrots, condensed milk, chocolate, the radio with its batteries, and all of the equipment collected from one encampment to the next by himself and his cooks.

St. Menoux paced around and around the cart. He opened his mouth to speak at least twenty times, finally remaining silent, realizing it would be useless.

By the end of the afternoon the little cart had absorbed a load which would have overburdened even a truck. As they were stretching the tarp over it, the sergeant arrived, shivering, coughing, a cigarette on his ear. The regiment truck refused to move. The radiator had frozen solid and burst. They would have to transfer its contents to the kitchen cart—twelve boxes of records, state forms, matriculation reports,

inkwells and pens, trunks belonging to the captain and the
lieutenants, canteens, the folding bed and the suitcases of the
accountant-sergeant.

St. Menoux raised his arms in despair and bit the ends of
his thin fingers through his fur gloves. The snowflakes fell
larger. The roofs of the farm were swallowed up in the gray
sky. The cooks swore. Credent cursed the sergeant, who
trudged through the snow and disappeared.

Soldiers brought up the extra baggage. Miraculously it all
fit on top of the provisions. A tarp covered the enormous
hump.

"I only have to hitch up the lead horse," said Polinet.

The snow softened the twilight, lending a solidity to the
still air. Two men at each wheel and two more behind
helped the horse start moving. The animal was old, toothless and half-blind, with a dirty, mangy coat. When the
weather was this cold, Polinet never took him out without
protecting his bad eye with a patch cut from his blue wool
coat. A great friendship had grown up between the peasant
and the old horse. The war had torn them both from their
normal labors, plunging them into the same ungodly misery.
They clung together like unfortunate brothers. The man
forged ahead with great strides. The horse panted, heaved
and pulled. To follow his master he would pull a mountain.

The equipment was to join the rest of the battalion at the
edge of the village. Together they would reach the station of
Tremplin-le-Haut, about twenty miles away, and embark
from there. Other vehicles had been waiting for an hour,
and the snow was rapidly covering them.

"The canteen! Good God, the canteen!" shouted St. Menoux. "What is Pilastre waiting for? He'll be the last one
again."

"There he comes," said Credent quietly. Pilastre pulled
up with his two horses, leading them by a long rope. He
mistrusted them. He was a metal-turner by vocation; his
boss had promised to take him back at the factory after the

war. He knew nothing about horses. He did not like animals. He was in the wrong place. He was fuming.

The animals didn't care for him either. One flame-colored, the other black, they hated each other as much as they feared him. Harnessing them was not a simple matter. Pilastre struck them on the muzzles with his fist. The horses reared back, snorting and looking to bite each other.

The canteen was a kind of battleship, a monument of iron and steel, assembled with three thousand rivets, carried on four iron wheels with large spokes as thick as thighs. In the middle of the courtyard Pilastre and his two horses danced their angry ballet. Behind them the four cooks, helmets on their heads and guns slung across their backs, their coats black with grease, were stirring up the fire. They threw log after log into the crackling hearth, above which steamed two enormous kettles of soup and the coffee for the trip.

Pilastre hoisted himself onto the seat. Wrapping himself in three blankets and raising his whip, he began to strike. The snow flew, the chains clattered and the tongue of the cart creaked. The canteen did not move. Each animal strained toward his own side, nullifying the other's effort with its own.

Credent removed his pipe from his mouth and spit. "What a bastard! Those damn animals—"

The driver stood erect and doubled the blows, hatred hollowing his cheeks and eyes. By accident the eight hoofs planted themselves simultaneously in the snow. The canteen took off like a shot, throwing Pilastre back into his seat. The two powerful horses charged across the courtyard at full gallop. With the roar of an express train, the canteen jumped over a heap of frozen manure, tore through the entrance gate and tipped over in the ditch, breaking the zero-mile record.

The fire of the hearth was scattered, hissing, across the snow. The cyclone had upset the soup and coffee, spilling them together. Ladles in their hands and brandishing their pokers, the cooks ran shouting toward the devastation. Credent ran behind them, cursing. St. Menoux, running behind Credent, plunged into the night along a road of smoking charcoal. The curtain of snow closed behind him.

Thus he began the voyage that was to lead him so far.

At the Tremplin-le-Haut station, the Pyrenean hunters set out without soup or coffee. They had waited for the convoy of trucks and food until around ten o'clock. The convoy had still not arrived when, at midnight, the first train left.

One by one the iron wheels of the vehicles had broken through the snow, reaching the underlayer of ice and softly slipping into the ditch. For one wagon in distress, the entire caravan had to grind to a halt. The sergeant, leader of the convoy, would run, waving his blazing signal light. Twenty men would pull at the wheels. The procession would move ahead another hundred meters before another wagon went down.

After nine hours of walking, stopping and hauling, the convoy pulled into Tremplin-le-Haut. The town was sleeping, its shutters guarding the warmth of the houses. The equipment trundled noiselessly over the snow-covered pavement. The station was at the far end of the town, at the top of a steep hill. The first car approached the incline, climbed about five yards and slid down again.

The leader of the convoy ordered four couples of horses unharnessed. The eight animals pulled the lead wagon up to the station, descended again and retrieved the next one. At this rate, dawn arrived before the final vehicle.

The weary men sat on the runningboards, leaned on the cart-shafts and crouching or standing, fell asleep. The tired horses hung their heads. The relentless snow began to bury the caravan.

St. Menoux, overcome with fatigue and loneliness, plodded on into the gray night, along the column, past the statuary horses, the phantom wagons to which clung the hazy silhouettes of men. His breath had frozen his Balaklava helmet to his beret, which was pulled down over his head like a nightcap. Behind the helmet, the cold cracked his lips. The studs of his ankle boots chilled his feet. The cold climbed along his calves, slipping sharply under his shoulder blades, gnawing at his sides and crushing his gloved fingers into his pockets.

His back hunched under the weight of the night, St. Menoux trudged past the lead truck and attacked the steep ascent, burying his feet in the deep snow. He heard the soft infinite fall of the snowflakes stretching out to an imagined horizon, out to the edge of the world.

Suddenly his foot struck something and he stumbled, almost falling. Peering ahead into the gloom he saw a stairway whose three steps climbed toward a door. He sighed. The black hole of the opening looked like a welcome shelter, a refuge from the storms around him. He climbed the steps and sat down on the top one, huddled in a ball, no longer able to move.

A car suddenly appeared at the bottom of the hill. Its headlights bleached the night, thousands of snowflakes dancing in the cone of light. The ground was like a vast outspread sheet. The auto slowed as it approached the summit, finally stopping completely. It could go no further. The motor sputtered, a door slammed. An officer covered with braids and stripes stepped into the light. The snow turned to gold. The officer opened his mouth to shout orders to his chauffeur, but the snow ate his words. St. Menoux heard nothing. He had no desire to hear. He was content. He no longer felt his feet nor his back.

The automobile softly began to back up, sliding back down the incline. The officer waved his gold-braided arms, dancing and running after the light which was slipping away more and more quickly. He grew smaller and smaller, finally disappearing completely into the cold.

St. Menoux slipped into sleep. His flesh ceased its suffering. He became light, insensitive, like a feather in the middle of a universe stuffed with soft cotton. Suddenly he fell backward. The door behind him had opened. Heat rushed out from the open passage, enveloped him and was lost in the chill of the street. A rectangle of sun was drawn on the snow. St. Menoux rose with great effort and turned around. A dark girl, young and beautiful, was standing before him like an apparition. In her hand she held a lamp. The light flowed along her hair, down onto her shoulders and shone from her large black eyes. She motioned to him to enter. He followed and the door closed on the night.

For weeks and weeks he had lived outside during the day and in the stable during the night. He had forgotten how men live in houses. His feet left puddles on the tiles of the entrance. The studs of his shoes squeaked. He felt heavy as a bear. The girl was looking at him, her face drawn with simple lines and bathed in peace. He flushed with embarrassment, but she only smiled kindly, without speaking.

He followed her into a room whose walls, floor and furniture shone softly in the glow of a lamp veiled with pink lace. An old round table of blond cherrywood barely touched the floor with its slender feet. Seated in a wheelchair, between the table and the earthenware stove, a man clothed in gray looked at St. Menoux.

"Hello, sir," said St. Menoux through his helmet.

The man was looking at him and shaking his head. He was enormous. His belly spread the arms of the chair, and his thighs pushed out to the left and right. A golden fan-shaped beard rose to the edge of his bald head, hiding his cheeks, his mouth, and his entire lower face, spreading out over his chest in billowing waves which shone in the light of the lamp like the tanned wood of the table. His pink and shiny baldness glowed like the enamel finish of the stove. A short white piece of string drew a crescent around his chin, buried in the golden sea of hair.

From the legs of his gray pants, deformed by the fat thighs and knees, emerged ankles as round as trees. At the extremities of these ankles there were no feet. Two stumps, covered with green knit socks, were resting on a leather cushion. The man buried his hand in his beard, drew out a pair of glasses, placed them on the end of his nose, which barely protruded from the mass of hair, and fell back into his chair.

St. Menoux sneezed. His cloak was dripping in a steamy ring around him.

A wave split the blond beard in two, revealing a snowy white smile. His eyes magnified by the glasses revealed a lively intelligence and a somewhat ironic benevolence.

"I've been waiting for you, Mr. St. Menoux. I have known for three months that you would come tonight to sit on the doorstep of my house, and I am delighted. I know still more —that your convoy will not begin to leave until 5:38 A.M. You have time to take off your coat, to refresh yourself and to listen to me. After you have heard me out, there will be time for everything."

The corporal, Master of Arts in Mathematics, heard only these astonishing words, that he had time to undress and to sit down. He did not need to be asked twice.

He began to unharness himself, undoing his suspenders and safety clasps, laying aside his rifle, water bottle, knapsack, gun-shield, shovel, bayonet, belt, cloak, gloves, helmet and beret. He immediately lost two thirds of his volume. He was so thin that his tall frame looked even more gaunt. His jacket could have enveloped four torsos like his, but the sleeves did not reach his wrists.

He stood somewhat hunched, perhaps from the habitual fear of striking the head of a door or a ceiling. His blue eyes were very pale, his nose and lips thin. He passed a long hand with thin fingers through his light blond hair, which the beret had plastered down.

The girl laid his equipment on the back of an armchair near the stove. Wearing pink satin slippers, she moved around the room silently. She placed the objects with efficient gestures, neither sluggishly nor with nervous haste. St. Menoux, deprived since childhood of a woman's care, followed her with his eyes, admiring her silent grace. He felt his embarrassment melt away. She brought him a chair and placed a bowl of coffee before him. He sat down and drank. She sat down in turn, just far enough away from him to watch him without disturbing him. She wore a white dress and looked to be about fifteen years old.

"She probably hasn't finished growing yet," St. Menoux thought to himself.

She looked tranquilly into his eyes. She was a child who did not know shame.

The invalid took a tortoiseshell-handled brush from the table and absentmindedly brushed his golden beard.

"Hmmm, he murmured. Perhaps we have looked at each other long enough! Now that you have seen us, allow me to introduce ourselves. Annette is my daughter. My name is Noel Essaillon."

"Noel Essaillon!" exclaimed St. Menoux, stupefied. "Let me see . . . It is you—it's you who answered me in February 1939 in *Mathematics Review*."

The man nodded and smiled, visibly pleased with the corporal's surprise.

"What a fascinating reply!" said St. Menoux, his astonishment turning to joy. "You are the man whom I have always wanted to meet."

He rose, forgetting his sufferings, his timidity, the war, the strangeness of his arrival at this place. He was again the abstract man, the passionate mathematician whose theories a year earlier had scandalized the scientific world. No one had understood him except this man, Noel Essaillon, whose remarks had opened new vistas to his mind.

He clasped his hands with emotion. The invalid seemed as happy as he.

"The war interrupted your works," said the large man. "I was able to continue mine and with sensational results. But you must be hungry, my friend, having struggled so far along the road. Annette . . ."

The girl excused herself, returning in a few minutes with a steaming omelette, a cold half-chicken, cheese, a pie and a bottle of Alsatian wine.

"Eat! Eat!" said Essaillon warmly, "and listen to me. What I am about to tell you is not ordinary."

St. Menoux did not need to be prodded.

"You are a mathematician and I am a physicist and chemist. I have been involved, for my part, in some research which would have resulted in nothing had your articles in *Mathematics Review* not enlightened me. Thanks to you, I was able to overcome certain obstacles which seemed insurmountable. The result is this: I have developed a substance which allows me to command time at my discretion."

St. Menoux put down his fork, but the large man would not give him time to interrupt. He animatedly continued his story. At times he seized his beard like a bunch of flowers, separating it in two and rubbing it between his fingers. Or he would stop to take a breath, his short breathing, along with the crackling of the smoldering fire, the only noise in the otherwise silent room.

His daughter was behind him in the shadows. She sat straight in the chair, her hands placed flat on her knees, grave as a child who is listening to a story. She was looking at the two men, each in turn, but especially at the new visitor, the tall thin soldier with the fair hair. From time to time she got up noiselessly to wipe her father's forehead or to change the visitor's plate. And none of that seemed for her work or habit. To awake on a new day, to go to town, to come back laden with white bread and vegetables, to eat, to walk, to notice the neighbors passing by, to listen to the cry of the woodseller and to work in the laboratory—this was her life. It was never gray or banal—in this aura of warm light, in sun or in snow, with bare trees or bouquets of foliage alive with birds.

St. Menoux, engrossed with his host's account, did not acknowledge her eyes upon him, but he felt the presence of the girl in the room like that of a precious object, a statue gilded with ancient gold which glows softly in a shadowy niche or a tapestry whose embroidered characters dance a woolen farandole upon a wall.

"Where do we come from?" continued Essaillon. "Where were we before our birth into the consciousness of this world? Religions speak of a lost paradise. Its regret haunts men of every race. This lost paradise I name the total universe. It is the universe that neither time nor space limit. It does not consist of three or four dimensions, but of every dimension. The light which illuminates it is composed, not of seven, or twenty, or one hundred, but of infinite colors. All that is, has been or will be, and all that will ever be, inhabits it. Nothing finds itself formed there, because all forms are possible within it. It occupies the atom and the infinite cannot fill it. For the soul that participates in this universe, the future or the past do not exist, nor the near or the far. All is presence to it."

St. Menoux had forgotten his meal. He saw, as in a dream, Annette's white hands pouring him a draft to drink and placing the food on his plate.

"Try to imagine now," Essaillon went on, "the sin against perfection for which this soul was condemned to the fall. It is involved in what we call 'life.' For the soul it is a kind of corridor, a vertical tunnel, whose material walls hide the memory of the marvelous journey. That soul can neither go back nor wander to the right or the left. It is inexorably attracted onward toward death, toward the end, toward the extremity of the tunnel which opens God knows where—into some frightful hell or to the rediscovered paradise. This soul is you, is me, during our terrestrial life. We who tumble in a free fall through time, like sand pebbles sifting through the fingers of God."

He raised his beard and dropped it to emphasize the image. It softly regained its harvest appearance.

St. Menoux drank the last drops of the clear wine.

"If I succeed," said Essaillon, "in changing the density of this soul, this pebble, it will be possible for me to either accelerate its fall or to stop it. I will even be able to free it from the power of gravity which attracts it to the future and to make it go back into the past. A means of accom-

plishing this intervention has been the goal of my work for
twenty years. And I have succeeded!"

He took the handkerchief from his daughter's hands,
mopped his brow and his neck, and added in a calmer voice,
"I imagine that this seems incredible to you. Therefore, before continuing, I would like to give you a demonstration."

He separated the gold curtain of hair which masked his
chest, revealing a woolen vest with pockets swollen like ud-
ders. His fingers probed among the objects within, settling
on a flat box which he held out to St. Menoux. He lifted the
cover and saw an assortment of tiny spheres of various colors,
laying on a bed of cotton.

"If you eat one of these pills," said Essaillon, "you will
immediately be restored to youth. By an hour, a day, a
week, a month, or a year, according to its color." He drew a
second box from his pocket. It contained other pills, oblong
in shape. "These ovules produce the opposite effect. They
accelerate your advance into the future."

He chose two violet pills and two ovules of the same
color from the box and placed them before St. Menoux:

"Try the experiment."

"Me?" asked the corporal, stupefied.

"Yes. This is the only way I have of convincing you.
Here you have all that is necessary to return into the past
for a period of two hours and to return immediately if you
wish. What have you decided?"

St. Menoux looked at the round fingers of the invalid as
they pushed the pills toward him across the clear wood of
the table. He felt flush with indecision, as if someone had
proposed a forbidden game. This man must be mad.

He raised his eyes toward the lamp and looked at the
things it touched with its light: the fine furniture, this wheez-
ing man, the daughter whose black eyes looked at him so
seriously. In her calm eyes, he saw the doubled image of the
bourgeois lamp. The startling words he had just heard con-
trasted with these seemingly ordinary surroundings. His scientific mind had easily followed the narration of his host, but

his common sense refused to accept the conclusions. Perhaps these pills contained poison? Perhaps they were only candy from the corner grocery.

Still he had been welcomed into this house with such strange words! He did not know what to believe anymore. His hesitation amused his host, who began to laugh. His belly shook from top to bottom, shaking his gray vest.

Abruptly, St. Menoux decided and placed his gaunt hand on the four pills. His curiosity had outweighed his fear.

"Very good," said Essaillon. Annette brought an envelope. St. Menoux slipped the two ovules into it, put it into his pocket, picked up the round pills and swallowed them.

He suddenly felt pulled from the back by a powerful force. He sprang from his chair, the light grew dim, a door slammed, a bitter wind roared in his ears, a howling wind filled with oaths and cries and the sound of a thousand hoofs. The snow raked his face. His feet and fingers were suddenly numb with cold. He wanted to cough. He sneezed. From the top of his canteen, Pilastre called to him,

"Corporal! Do you think we'll get there tonight?"

"We will get there when we can, my friend."

Before these words left his mouth, he recognized them. He had already answered the same question with the same words before. He waited for the response of the driver. The "shit" arrived exactly on its quarter-second.

The convoy proceeded into the night. One mile ahead lay Tremplin-le-Haut and St. Menoux knew that it would take more than an hour to cover these few thousand feet and that they would stop four times before reaching the sleeping city. One driver lit his pipe. In the match light crossed with snowflakes, the corporal of the echelon saw a purple nose and two ice cubes hanging on a moustache. He had already seen the same face. But this time, to the face of the man from Auvergne, his memory compared another face, the face of a young girl lit by a pink lamp.

He began to relive two hours of his existence. Second by

second, step by step, he relived again the events which he
remembered. A tremendous exultation overcame him, driv-
ing the cold from his flesh. It seemed to him that he advanced surrounded by light. The night, the cold, the suffering,
the filth, the stupid ignorance of the future toward which one
proceeds like a blind man, all that was the concern of other
men, of the herd. He felt light and powerful, like a demigod,
as different from his drivers as they from their mules.

A thought suddenly struck him. Just suppose, he said to
himself, I change my route? Suppose I were to pass by without stopping in front of the three steps of the wizard's house?
I am free to choose. I can avoid the events I foresee, alter
my destiny and still remain a soldier like the others for whom
time is measured by the accumulation of sufferings. I could
embark with the troops without seeing Noel Essaillon! In
reality he could go no further. Curiosity had overcome him
and nothing in the world could keep him from following out
the experiment.

He was anxious to know more, to leave this snow and
cold, this trudging journey. He looked for the accelerating
pills, blinked his eyes under the falling snowflakes and shook
the envelope between his lips.

The pills slipped onto his tongue. His muscles contracted
in anticipation of the shock. He swallowed with a gulp of
saliva. He felt the pills descend his esophagus. They settled,
warm and luminous, in his stomach. Their light radiated
through him, filling the room around him. Noel Essaillon was
looking at him, somewhat mockingly it seemed. Above the
great man's shoulder, he saw the face of the smiling girl
whose eyes seemed to him so full of sweetness. He smiled in
return.

"Here I am—back," he said. "Did you have to wait long?"

"You just left," replied the invalid. "You left us with an
anguished face and you return with a smile. We hardly had
time to notice that your chair was empty. I won't ask you if
you are convinced."

St. Menoux rose to shake Essaillon's hand. He wanted to

hug him, but he thought that would look ridiculous. He did not succeed in suppressing his excitement altogether. He knocked over a cup with his jacket coattails. Annette was laughing as he apologized.

"Pull yourself together, my dear friend," said Essaillon. "Your perplexity touches me more than your compliments. I am very happy to see you are so enthusiastic. How can one not be, it is true, after such an experience. Now do you understand the value of my discovery? Reaching forty years of age, you decide to begin your life again. You return to your adolescence. You launch out into life with a brand-new body in a new existence. You avoid the misfortunes which struck you in your first existence. You seize all of the good fortune that eluded you. You begin again one hundred times, one thousand times. You are in possession of all the sciences in the world, speak all languages. You have loved all women and are familiar with all your contemporaries. You have seen all, heard all and known all. You are God!"

Essaillon again was overcome with excitement. He seemed ready to rise up, to break away like an athlete from his deformed body.

"Someday, perhaps," he continued, "tired of this earthly eternity, you will let yourself be carried to death, which will be the only knowledge which you will not have tasted."

"If my eyes are not deceiving me, you have not 'begun again' yourself," St. Menoux remarked. His eyes went from the obese man's face, to his stomach, to his truncated legs.

The invalid's exuberance faded. He sank into his armchair and fell silent for a few seconds. Then he began again in a low voice. "No. No, I could not. I have made short voyages into the past. I return from them each time to continue my research. But I have not changed my destiny. I haven't had the courage.

"No doubt it seems to you that I have no need of courage to leave this deformed carcass, that on the contrary I should have abandoned it with pleasure. But to do that I would have to change my heart. I could not deliberately separate myself from my child. I did not wish to avoid the accident that made me an invalid. It is thanks to it that I found Annette's mother. She was my nurse. We married. She died on the day she gave birth to this treasure."

He held out his arms. The sleeves of his vest, shortened by the folds at the elbows, revealed his round wrists, white as a baby's bottom. His daughter came to kneel near him, placing her head on his knees. Essaillon tenderly caressed the brown locks which mixed with the golden flow of his beard.

"These ties have bound me to the present," he said. "I could not imagine life in which my child would no longer be at my side."

St. Menoux nodded. "I understand."

Essaillon again spoke with the clear voice of a scientist. "I let myself be carried away a moment ago by my dreams," he said. "In reality, I do not believe that a man possessing my pills, no matter how egotistical or determined he might be, could freely use them. He would always find a love or a hatred to enchain him. Besides, it is not the secret of immortality or of the all-powerful that I am searching. I am not working for myself but for mankind.

"I have also explored the future," he continued, "but with extreme caution, since I don't know where death is waiting for me. I did not go far. I feared each minute that I might go beyond my lifespan. In short, my invention, which excites you so, doesn't really satisfy me. This substance, to which I have given the name 'noelite,' operates only within the limits of our existence. It does not allow us to leave this tunnel through which we are falling toward death, to leap into infinite time while retaining our present personalities. That is what interests me. My pills can only serve my egotistical designs. I dream of being useful to humanity. I don't know if that will be possible. Men have always refused the aid of one who offered to lead them from their pain and have followed instead in the path of those who led them into misfortune. Still, still . . ."

He fell silent for a moment. His green eyes, flooded with

dreams, followed some astounding vision. He passed his fleshy hand across his brow, saying in a low voice, "It is not presumptuous of me to hope that after having traveled through the centuries, studied at its source past and future history, sought out the exact causes of wars, revolutions and great miseries, that it may be possible to avoid some of them. Perhaps we could accelerate progress, borrow from our grandsons some inventions or reforms which brought them happiness, in order to offer them to our grandfathers. Why not?"

He fell silent again. St. Menoux, overwhelmed by these words, no longer saw the invalid. He forgot the mutilated legs, the deformed stomach, the face which expressed as much skepticism as intelligence, the fat hands that bespoke a glutton. In his mind another image of Essaillon took form— a giant, standing triumphant, who held out his arms to the wretched multitude. A genius, the kind of person who appears now and again among men to change their destiny.

Essaillon struck the arm of his chair. "Yes," he said in a firm voice. "I must find a substance which will liberate us from the walls of our lifespan. I know that I will find it, but it will take a long time. How much time? It doesn't matter— I have eternity at my command. I can begin again indefinitely on any given day and make it last a century. In any case, I have chosen you to assist me in the explorations that I plan to undertake when I have succeeded. I am not asking for your answer. I know it. Your intelligence, your scientific nature, sister to my own, assures me of your cooperation. Already it is thanks to your articles that I was able to bring my previous work to some fruition, when otherwise it would have failed. From now on I am counting on you. Here is my plan."

He straightened himself in his chair. His beard flowed like a river. He wore a look of such gravity and nobleness that St. Menoux could not raise the slightest objection.

"You must not shy from your duty to the country. You will resume your life as a soldier. Go back into the night and the cold, serve in the war, knowing that you will emerge from it uninjured. Moreover, the noelite will permit you to pass through it so quickly that you will know it only as a memory.

"I am going to give you two one-year pills. Take them at the same time. In two years you will find yourself in Paris. I will join you there. While you are fighting the speedy war, I will have lived ten, one hundred, one thousand years—all the time necessary for the culmination of my research. Now it is time for you to leave us, to return to us later."

St. Menoux stood up, deeply moved. Annette held his cloak out to him. She had to raise her arms high to cover his shoulders with the steaming coat. He gave a last glance at the room where the pink mist floated, and then leaned over to place a kiss on the girl's hand.

He hesitated. One must not kiss young unmarried ladies' hands, he said to himself. On the other hand, I am not an ordinary man, but a soldier. He completed his gesture and plunged into the icy night. The swirling snow enveloped him.

In two years, he thought. The war will be over in two years.

He saw himself marching along the Champs-Elysees, his beret over his ear, after the great assault into the heart of the enemy nation. Then he realized that this was really of no importance. The task awaiting him loomed higher.

A snowflake flicked at his eyeball, causing him to close the lid. A frozen tear glued his eyelashes. The trampling of horses passed by him in the night, accompanied by cursing, the gnashing of harnesses and carriage shafts. He lowered his helmet and snatched up the two pills. They tickled his throat going down. He sneezed.

2

"What miserable weather!" he said. "And this window won't close!"

Crossing the small bedroom, he rubbed his hands together to warm them. A wool scarf wound around his neck three times and came up to his eyes. He pushed aside the navy blue curtain which covered the window and tried to tighten the shutters, caked with ice. A burst of cold air struck him in the stomach. He sneezed again and returned to sit at his white wooden table. A lamp with a newspaper for a lampshade was placed near the office calendar. The date was circled—February 21, 1942. It was one o'clock in the morning. February 22nd had begun. St. Menoux turned the sheet.

Two years had passed since the moment in the snow at Tremplin-le-Haut, when he had swallowed the noelite. Had they really passed with the speed predicted by Essaillon? From the snows of Champagne to the snows of Paris—had he leaped over those long months? He had such vivid memories of the alert on May 10, 1940; of the confidence with which he had entered Belgium; of the sky suddenly filled with planes, the bombs falling like hail, the crushed trucks; of six of his drivers dead and the retreat in disarray to the camp of Souges, near Bordeaux; of the flies that infested the excrement-filled camp, the dysentery and despair; of the departure for the Pyrenees, the demobilization; his replacement in Paris by the nonmobilized; his nomination to a provincial college and finally his return to the capital at the beginning of the year.

27

Certainly he had lived all that. He looked at himself in the mirror. He saw there the features of a man who had hardly learned to deal with the real. His face showed no mark of suffering. The night of Tremplin-le-Haut—had it been a dream? He closed his eyes and saw again the cripple with his beard of fire and his stomach, like a great gourd, in the chair. And the silent girl . . .

He did not know what to believe anymore. Corrected exams were spread across his desk: forty students of Advanced Math, aged eighteen to twenty. He had spent part of the night on their homework. The night—two years? One second? Just time to swallow? Time? What was time? On the papers sat a small silver object, a souvenir of his stay at the Essaillon's, a teaspoon taken inadvertently.

He took it in his hand. It was icy cold. Shivering, he undressed, retaining his woolen underwear and slipping on a none-too-clean pair of pajamas. A bachelor's pajamas. He sat down on his bed. His grasshopper knees folded under his chin, he felt the cold sheets with the ends of his toes, and slipped into the bed as into an icy river. He could not warm himself. He missed the straw of the stable at Vanesse, the heat and the odor of horses. That memory seemed very close to him. Like yesterday.

He heard the clock strike three, then four. The hours never end. Had he traveled through two years in a lightning flash? The winter wind wailed through the sleeping city. In the next room Mr. Michelet, his neighbor, snored.

If Essaillon kept his promise, he would arrive today. Essaillon and his daughter Annette.

He awoke to a rapping on his door. He shouted, "Okay, okay, I'm coming!" It's them, he thought.

He leaped out of bed. Halfway to the door he remembered his freezing feet, went back to his bed and slipped on his socks. His teeth chattered with emotion and from the cold. Wrapping a blanket around himself, he ran to open the door.

"Mr. St. Menoux?" a high melodious voice greeted him. He looked down. At the height of his belt buckle he saw the cap and red nose of a telegraph boy.

"Yes, that's me."

"Here you are, sir."

The boy held out a telegram in a mittened hand. Then he turned on his heel and rushed down the stairs, singing, "Baby, I want your love . . ."

St. Menoux heard his landlady in the hall. His hands were trembling. The return address read: Noel Essaillon, 7, Racine Villa, Paris 16.

MY DEAR FRIEND,

WE HAVE RETURNED FOR THE RENDEZVOUS. WE AWAIT YOU FOR LUNCH.   SINCERELY, NOEL ESSAILLON

"Well, my dear neighbor. I hope it is good news!"

Startled at hearing himself addressed, Peter realized that he was still standing on the threshold of his room. He shut the door, muttering, "Thank you. Thank you." Locks of his pale hair fell across his eyes.

Mr. Michelet shrugged his shoulders and went down to breakfast. An unhappy architect, Michelet, by the time he was fifty, had lost all of his clients and most of his fortune. He lived in this furnished house on St. James Boulevard because on the other side of the boulevard a building of his design was under construction. It was a kind of chalet with turrets and bell towers surrounded by about five feet of a garden of sorts and squeezed between a furniture warehouse and a coal depot. From his bedroom window overlooking the subway, Mr. Michelet could contemplate his masterpiece during the day.

It was the only happiness that remained for him. Age and misfortune had shriveled him. His store-bought clothes seemed too large. His gray felt hat, turning a dirty brown, came down over his ears. His face had lost all color. Even his eyes were a vague color, like a pool where the muddy bottom is seen among a few reflections of the sky. In his youth, his moustache must have been triumphant. Now it

fell limply parallel to the bitter corners of his mouth and
down to his poorly shaven chin. It was gray on the ends and
the color of a cigarette butt all along the lip.

To avenge the spitefulness of destiny, Mr. Michelet told
his misfortunes to everyone. He clung to hotel tenants and
people he chanced to meet who did not know better than to
lend an ear to his tales of woe. He began each morning by
pouring out his feelings to the customers of the Bougnat bar
where he drank his national coffee.

He arrived, impatient, before sunrise, as the percolator
began to whistle. The owner yawned as he aligned the
stemmed glasses jingling with little spoons on the counter.
He always found the same shivering workmen who would
take one of the early subways. His gabardine coat wedged
itself against the bar between their threadbare overcoats and
blue jeans. The plumber passed him the squirt of saccharine
that replaced the regretted cognac, giving him an amiable tap
on the back and asking if "things weren't coming along better?" Then Mr. Michelet began to recount his misfortunes.
Occasionally some impolite character interrupted him, saying, "We've already heard your song." Even if they said nothing, they were not listening to him. They let him speak.
They talked about the war. Each one knew how it was going to end.

An alley opened between two houses in the icy air. It
left the bourgeois street and was lost among the trees. Two
walls set with rare doors and iron gates ran along each side,
covered with a layer of snow pierced by pointed iron spikes.
Some steps marked a path on the white blanket which covered the sidewalks. The trees intertwined their naked
branches high in the sky. A forest silence bathed this patch
of nature forgotten in the city.

St. Menoux had to look for the numbers under the inter-
laced roots of ivy. He noticed some isolated houses through
the trunks and clumps of trees. At No. 5, three wolf-dogs
rushed from the further end of the park and threw them-

selves against the door. They jumped at the iron gate as he passed, growling savagely, their open jaws reaching for him between the bars.

No. 7 was the last iron gate, a double door which closed on the end of the alleyway. St. Menoux rang the bell. Footsteps crossed the snow. An aged woman appeared. She was wearing a white headpiece with large starched wings and a black dress closed up to the neck.

"Does Mr. Essaillon live here?"

She nodded yes without saying a word. The wings of her cap fluttered. She made a sign to the visitor to follow her. Then she was running, the pleats of her skirt flying around her white cotton stockings.

St. Menoux, surprised, ran behind her along a path and climbed the flight of steps of a freestone house. She did not give him time to recover his composure as she drew aside two doors.

Peter stood panting, trying to catch his breath. He was welcomed by Annette's laugh. "Obviously," he said, "I could never—make a normal entrance—at your house!"

He remembered his wet boots on the floor at Tremplin-le-Haut. This was the same room, the same furniture, illuminated by a similar light, coming from the windows veiled with pink curtains. Seated in the same chair, the invalid, his two hands on his beard, watched St. Menoux enter with the same benevolent and slightly ironic smile. Behind him, his daughter remained standing. She alone had changed. She had bloomed, but kept in her eyes that pure flame which shines in the eyes of very young children or those who have nothing to hide. She had grown up in isolation, near this father who was content to revel in her concern, her help and her beauty. No one had taught her to see evil where there was none.

She took a few steps toward St. Menoux. She was clothed in a pleated navy blue skirt with suspenders over a lace bodice. She walked, her arms half-folded, her hands outstretched. She held out her hands and milky arms to the

visitor. With each step, her free breasts swayed behind the
lace. Her skirt surrounded her delicate waist, encircled her
full hips and danced around her perfect legs. Two locks of
hair fell in brunette swirls across her temples. Some wild
wisps shadowed her forehead and nape of her neck, catching
the light that surrounded her head. Her pink and golden complexion evoked the warmth of blood and sun. She was smiling, without opening her lips, the same smile that had welcomed St. Menoux two years earlier, which bathed her in
sweetness and mystery.

St. Menoux scarcely knew how to appreciate feminine
beauty. He lived mainly in the mind, in those inhuman re-
gions where mathematics lead a few privileged beings. As
for Annette, he recalled her luminous face and the warm
welcome she had given him. He did not separate her from
the memory of her father.

He was overcome by the beauty and manner of the girl,
but when he held her hand, he no longer thought of her. He
was the prey of an anguished curiosity.

At the moment when the young man's hand touched on
hers, Annette suddenly stopped smiling. She turned around
slowly to watch him walk away from her, advancing across
the room toward her father.

"We are very happy to see you again, my dear friend,"
said the invalid. "I hope that my old Philomena did not
receive you too badly. She's my daughter's nurse. You could
not meet her during your first visit. She was dead."

These last words freed St. Menoux from his anguish. It
seemed like a good joke. He began to laugh.

"That's something new," he said. "One can always expect a
surprise around you."

"Oh, that is not so surprising! Sit down, my dear St.
Menoux. You know the devotion of these old domestics.
Philomena used to manage the house. So that "nothing would
be wasted," she used to eat the leftovers. One day she poisoned herself, no doubt with some piece of meat that she
had left too long in the pantry. She died in fifteen days. An-

nette cried over her. A terrible grief. When the noelite was ready, I found Philomena again in the past and attempted to prevent her from dying. But I could not find the exact cause of her illness. Not knowing what had poisoned her, I locked her in her room and forbade her to eat for eight days, then one week with bread and water. She came out of it very thin and half mad, but alive. Since then, she has never left us."

"She must be terribly grateful."

"Don't believe it," answered Essaillon. "On the contrary, she won't forgive me for it. She lives in perpetual remorse for my having "stolen her time." She hurries, she runs in the hope of finishing this stolen life more quickly. My new experiments hardly please her. She says that the devil possesses me."

His eyelids, folded over, almost entirely hid his eyes. Peter was astonished to see a shadow of anger pass over his face.

Even before the war St. Menoux, held back by his budget, had never eaten such a meal. Lobster, chicken, leg of lamb, fresh peas, asparagus, and salad followed one after another across his plate. And to top it off, after a choice of creamy cheeses and butter cookies, he was served strawberries, cherries and grapes of unbelievable freshness in the middle of February.

He had a small stomach. The miniscule portions at the restaurants of Category D had always sufficed him. He paid too little attention to eating. When he did notice a meal it was to suffer, like his neighbors, from the dull foods of the armistice.

Philomena's kitchen seemed to awake in him the faculty of taste. He marveled at each out-of-season delicacy. He stuffed himself with the first course and so could only taste the others. The white bread, ordinarily a treat, seemed dull to him. He smelled the coffee arriving before the maid had placed the cups on the table.

Essaillon reveled in his newly discovered taste buds, Annette in his pleasure.

The invalid ate for four and drank hard. His beard was

filled with crumbs. He shook it after each course. His appetite seemed habitual. Seeing his daughter refill his plate, St. Menoux guessed that she must serve him as copiously for each meal. Essaillon confirmed this openly to his guest.

"You see," he said, "I am at heart an ingenuous person. I can never have enough of the joys of this world—joys of the senses, of the heart and of the mind. It hurts me to see so many unhappy men around me when life could offer them such great and varied pleasures. Today I am the only one able to eat fruits ripened in their normal time and gathered in winter. But soon I hope everyone will be able to do the same. Come, I want to show you where I store these riches."

Annette pushed her father's wheelchair. All three entered a neighboring room, which reminded St. Menoux of a bank vault. Its walls were divided into a number of little metal gray doors, each one with a knob and a white button similar to that of a doorbell. The invalid seized one of the knobs and pulled. The hinged door opened into blackness. The light from the large windows did not penetrate an inch into the coffer. It seemed full of obscurity as though of a solid substance. The eye fell upon a total shadow, unable to perceive even the palest reflection. In a room opened to the afternoon light, this rectangle was irrational.

"Put your hand in the safe," said Essaillon.

St. Menoux approached cautiously, reached out his arm and mumbled. His hand could not enter the void. It met with no resistance. He groped at the darkness with his fingertips. He felt nothing, no smooth or rough grain. No matter. No sensation of temperature. Nothing. There was no surface there at all. Yet his hand, which nothing stopped, could not go further. Then he put both hands into the door. He felt like a burglar groping for the secret of a lock. His fingers felt along the void. He leaned against the opening, his entire body supported by his hands placed flat against the blackness. His hands were in contact with nothing. He was leaning against nothingness.

Essaillon had pulled his glasses from the pocket of his

wool vest, placing them on his nose. His eyes danced behind them.

"Do not persist, my dear Peter," he said. "First of all, I am going to show you the content of this cupboard. I shall then explain the mystery to you. Watch!"

He pressed the white button. St. Menoux saw the obscurity tremble, swirl and dissolve. A green lamp had begun to shine onto the ceiling from the cupboard. Its pale light lit four pats of butter placed on wooden trays. St. Menoux put out his hand. It went in this time without difficulty and his index finger made a hole in the butter.

While Peter was sheepishly licking his finger, Essaillon leaned on the button a second time. A black fog veiled the lamp, stopped level with the door and lay there like a block. The invalid closed the hinged door.

"You have seen my pantry," he said. "Now I shall explain how it functions."

They returned to the next room. Philomena had placed an assortment of alcoholic beverages on the table.

"Choose what you like and help yourself. You have just seen an application of noelite. I have succeeded in manufacturing a new variety of this substance. In my desire to remain near my cherished daughter as long as possible, I wished to eternalize the present. I obtained results very different from those I anticipated.

"What is the present in our little universe? While I think of the sentence that I shall say to you, it is already a part of the future. As I pronounce it, it falls into the past. Is the present the moment when I taste this marvelous liqueur? No! As long as it has not reached my lips, it is the future. When the sensation of its taste, its warmth which fills my mouth, when this pleasure reaches my brain, it has already left my palate. It is the past. The future drowns in the past as soon as it has ceased to be future. The present does not exist. To eternalize it would be to eternalize nothingness. That is what I have done!"

St. Menoux put down his glass. He did not even know what he had been drinking.

"Those cupboards that you saw are coated on the inside with a paint base of noelite 3. This paint removes whatever is inside the cupboard from the action of passing of time. The green lamp annuls the action of the noelite. I light the green lamp and put a live chicken in the cupboard. I turn off the lamp. The chicken ceases to be. The present, which doesn't exist for him, will thereafter be the unique form of his time. He no longer moves, because movement supposes quickness, departure and arrival, and the passing of time. His blood stops. His sensations no longer run through his nervous system. He remains fixed in the present. He can stay this way for a thousand years without growing old and without feeling. As soon as the green lamp is relit, he begins to exist again. A burning match can remain in my cupboard for an eternity without being consumed.

"What is the state of the objects or living organisms thus preserved in an eternal present? We can only guess. We can not discover through the senses because light, odor, sounds, all stop under the action of the noelite. If you can not make your hand enter the cupboard, it is because there can be no movement inside this perpetual present. Thus nothingness remains unknowable.

"When I created noelite 3, I returned to 1938 with Annette, bought this hotel and had these coffers built. I applied a coat of paint to them and supplied them with various provisions. When one of them is empty, Annette makes a tour back to before the war and fills it."

"It's so funny," said Annette, "to find myself again as a little girl with my experience as a woman!"

"Listen to her," said the invalid. "Listen to her speak of her experience, this youngster."

Peter looked at her. He tried to imagine the return of this magnificent adolescent in her body of a grown woman. He saw her breasts grow smaller, become flat, her calfs grow thin, her face grow hard . . . She looked into his eyes, and he turned his head away first. He coughed. "Truly with you the miraculous becomes habit. You walk through time as through the town streets. Have you found other uses for noelite 3?"

"Yes. I have coated the inside of the ticking of our mattresses, from which the wool has been removed. We sleep softly supported by nothingness. What an astonishing sensation to feel oneself lying on nothing. You see already what uses the new substance can be put to. Alas, the history of our time reveals to us that all inventions can be more easily used to bring misfortune to men than happiness. I wanted to ascertain for myself the harmfulness of noelite 3."

He put down his glass. A drop of Armagnac cognac shone near his lip, like a drop of light dew, between two golden threads.

"I have forwarded to a distant headquarters, by indirect means, about three hundred gallons of it in its liquid state, in special containers. I indicated the precautions to take in order to line active bombs. I asked that they send me the results by radiophonic broadcast in Sanscrit. There are not too many men who understand that language in today's world. Besides, those who do generally make fun of the wireless. That was six months ago. I fixed the hour and the day of the broadcast. I was waiting for you. It should be heard today, immediately. Let's listen."

He opened the door of an ancient carved chest. A slab of ebonite was furnished with milled buttons. When the first button was turned on, the radio growled indistinctly.

Essaillon searched for the wave length. A thread of blue light moved across the numbers of a dial. Echoes of the world sputtered into the room; a burst of brass instruments, three trills of a soprano, the staccato of the Morse code and the noise of jamming trains, all over the deformed voices of the speakers.

"There it is," said the scientist. He looked at the dial of a tall clock whose copper pendulum struck the time. "In two minutes."

The wireless gave out a strange station signal, five flute notes constantly repeated, magical as the music of a snake charmer.

St. Menoux, who had risen, sat down again softly on the edge of his chair. He did not dare to make any noise with his breathing. Annette, her hands on the table, looked at her father with anxiety. The two minutes passed.

"I wonder—" grunted the old man. He suddenly fell silent. A voice sounded from the wireless, a man's voice, sharp, monotonous, speaking incomprehensible words full of the chant of vowels. Essaillon's face lit up. He listened passionately. With his two hands, he made a sign to the others to be quiet; to cease all noise. Then he spoke in a low voice, in short broken phrases.

"They tried it—on a small city—somewhere in Asia—

St. Menoux felt his heart tighten. He had a premonition of the abominable. Annette's little hands closed on the table.

"One missile was sufficient. It is flying over the city, and delivers the bombs. They are bursting above the roofs. The noelite is falling like rain. No noise, no confusion. No blocks of houses reduced to dust. A few bombs only, bursting in the air with a dull sound. A little rain falling. The people raise their heads, see the sky streaked with black rays. The noelite is falling, the rain reaches beasts and men—reaches the ground. No blood, no burns. A little rain neither warm nor cold."

The voice on the wireless continued its story without emotion, like a litany. Little by little, Essaillon grew excited. No doubt he was imagining as he translated, replacing the abstract words of the ancient language with concrete phrases, adding what he guessed and what the stranger who was speaking so far away could not know.

"A black rain which does not wetten—a rain of invisible ink. The man who receives a few drops of it on his hand and wishes to raise it to his face notices with fright that he can no longer move his hand. It is nailed to the air, nailed to the immutable present. He can no longer move his head. He had noelite in his hair, on his shoulders. He is bound. He screams in terror. The entire city is howling. All living beings have been touched here and there. Each untouched part continues to grow while the other part is immobilized in time. In place of an arm, a nose, they have only a weightless shadow fixed in space like cement.

"The surface of the streets is strewn with spots. The houses are half phantoms. The trees along the avenues are covered with black leaves, which the winds no longer stir. A storm moves the river whose untouched water has to break its way through the solidified water. The air is full of millions of bars of darkness. Each drop of falling noelite has carried a thin pillar of shadow to the ground which no one can break nor free, it being only the thickness of a strand of hair. All which lives, all which ordinarily dies, is nailed with arrows to the immobile present.

"Men and beasts are dying because a principal artery is obstructed, because the nerves no longer command the life to continue. Those who are least touched know, after the sufferings of immobility, the sufferings of hunger and thirst. The streets are peopled with a crowd of ensnared beings who are struggling, trying in vain to tear themselves from this horror. In the houses, men and women preserved by the walls and roofs can no longer leave their homes. In the streets are erected prisons between whose bars it is impossible to slip. Hunger overcomes the beseiged.

"Soon death extends its silent hand over the city. In the streets, cadavers are hanging, fastened to the air by pieces of their flesh which the noelite has touched. Decay, little by little, tears them from their bodies. The ground is strewn with carrion, fleshless bone, while the air remains peopled with profiles, ears, heads of hair, breasts, black fingers, stiff, eternal, bound to the sky by the immobile rain of the present."

The wireless was silent for a few minutes. Essaillon was silent in turn. Removing his glasses, he wiped his hand over his forehead and eyes.

"It's horrible," said St. Menoux in a low voice.

"Yes, it's horrible," agreed the invalid. "Horrible—but fantastic, isn't it?"

His eyes, the color of the sea, shone with a peculiar exaltation. He went on, "Imagine that there exists perhaps in this city a man on whom enough noelite fell to preserve him entirely in the present. Perhaps a signalman on a roof near the bomb's explosion point. That man, alone in the silent city, neither living nor dead, continues to stand guard, outside of eternity. The end of the world will never touch him, because it will never reach him. Even God can no longer reach him . . ."

Annette sighed. "You should perhaps drink something," she said to St. Menoux in a sweet voice.

Without waiting for his answer, she poured him two fingers of wine. He decided that maybe she was less affected by the horror of the story, because she found herself more sensitive to joys than to misfortunes, to beauty than to ugly things. Her body, aglow with life, was attracted to life and her mind remained closed to images of death.

A great crash of broken dishes came from the direction of the kitchen.

"Oh dear," said Annette. "Poor Philomena is taking revenge on the china again."

She left the room. She was wearing blue suede shoes, very simple, with high heels, which made her bare ankles seem finer and which contracted a bit the outline of her calfs. She was humming the tune of the flute on the wireless. St. Menoux did not see her leave. He was wondering how he was going to say what was on his mind.

"I—hum," he said, clearing his throat. "I do not wish to reproach you, don't think that. I admire you very much. But I think you were perhaps wrong to give your invention to the military. Aren't you afraid they will wreak havoc?"

Essaillon ran the quail brush through his beard. The bristles caressed the hairs with a satin noise.

"Set your mind at rest, my little Peter," he said. "They

will have no more noelite. They don't know where it comes from and if they attempt to analyze it, they will only succeed in rendering useless their instruments, their laboratories and perhaps their chemists. A little while ago they offered me a lot of money. They added that they will call me back every day. I will not listen to them. It is a completed experiment.

"I guess that you are angry at me for having done it. It does not seem to you to agree with my humanitarian goals. It is, however, because of this experiment that I will never hand over my noelite to the public. Before acting, it is necessary to know. The Chinese who invented the powder for fireworks would perhaps have stopped his research if he had foreseen the cannon. On the other hand, we scientists must not show too much sentimentality. What is the death of a few thousand men when one works for the good of entire humanity?"

He threw the brush on the table with an offhand gesture. His eyes had become cold as a frozen pond. But St. Menoux could not forget the excitement he had seen shining in these same eyes during the account of the bombardment.

Essaillon rubbed his hands together and began to smile. He was once again the bon vivant, the gourmand, the happy scientist. "And now I shall show you my wonder, thanks to which you will soon be able to voyage in future centuries. Please be so kind as to push my wheelchair."

They proceeded to an adjoining room which must have been the laboratory. Four large tables of pink marble were arranged along the walls. A half-circle was cut into each one of them to allow the obese Essaillon to work there without leaving his chair. The surface of the tables was bare. Under each there were steel cupboards with closed doors. Above one table a uniform of green cloth was hanging on a nail. Essaillon pointed it out. "There is the object," he said. "Take it down."

St. Menoux spread out on the table a kind of coverall, in one piece from the hood to the pants. A zipper parted it down the front. Two holes were cut in it for the eyes. Two

similar openings were set into the material at the ear level.
The material seemed to have been dipped in a wash of
sulphate.

"Here are the necessary accessories," added Essaillon, who
drew from a cupboard a pair of boots, gloves with very
long cuffs, motorcycle glasses, and a leather belt to which
was fixed a square metal fitting, as large as those the Parisian
bus conductors carry on their belts.

He added two haversacks and a knapsack. Leather, metal
and glasses—all were equally green. "All this," said the
scientist, "is covered with a combination of noelite 3 and
noelite 1 and 2. When you have put on this uniform, put on
these glasses, and slipped on these gloves and boots, the device attached to your belt will allow you to walk through the
centuries. Switching it on activates both noelite 3 and one of
the two others, at your choice. You wish to move a hundred
years ahead? Noelite 2 will transport you there instantly.
Noelite 3 will preserve you as you are. It preserves your
present state while the others throw you into the future or
the past.

"Operating the device is very simple. These five buttons
allow you to move the index along the markings of the
hours, days, months, years and centuries. The middle of the
scale, marked with a zero, is the time of your departure.
To the left is the past, to the right, the future. With the
index set, you push this round button and you are immediately
transported to the point of time which you determined. To
return, push on this square button. There you are, brought
back to your point of departure like a rubber band.

"This triangular button starts a vibrator. You only set it
into motion upon your arrival. The vibrator makes your time
vary from one second ahead and behind, to a very rapid
rhythm. Through each coming and going, you jump over the
present. For the people who surround you, you are never
there, always late or ahead by one second in their time. You
are therefore invisible, untouchable. If a wall appears before
you, do not hesitate to cross through it. It cannot stop you

since you are not yet there, or already passed. Nothing is an obstacle to you.

"Don't forget, when you put on the glasses, to insert the earphones into these little holes. The glasses and earphones are, in fact, synchronized with the vibrator. As soon as the latter begins, the glasses and the membrane of the earphones vibrate in harmony with it, but in the opposite direction. They delay the light and sounds when your time is accelerated, and accelerate them when you are behind. They restore the world to you—without them you would only have a blurred, chaotic sensation of it. Perhaps there will be at times a slight fading effect in your hearing, and it may seem to you that your vision is dimmed. But your senses will adjust very quickly. Nothing will obstruct you and if you judge it safe to show yourself, you may stop the vibrator. One more push on the button will suffice. The haversacks contain provisions, arms, tools, a movie camera, and pieces of rubber cloth to rapidly repair any tear in the "diving suit of time." That's what I have named this uniform. The sack will allow you to bring back some objects or small living beings from your explorations."

St. Menoux was no longer astonished. "You keep saying 'you,'" he suddenly remarked. Aren't you coming with me?"

"Alas, how could I come?" answered the invalid, his brow darkening.

He pointed to his stumps. "I can't even stand."

"Well then, all this has not yet been tried?"

"Yes, by me," said Annette gaily, as she entered the room.

St. Menoux looked at her in astonishment. He would not have thought that she would take an active part in her father's research. His astonishment awoke his desire and he saw the young woman in a flash as she was, both frail and strong, her body firm and full, tender and radiant.

"You are so—" he began. He was going to say "so beautiful," but he was aware that his compliment was also an absurdity. He stopped and blushed.

"These trials have shown us," repeated the inventor, "that

the voyage in time is accompanied by a voyage in space. But if my apparatus commands the first, the second seems to be determined by desires or unconscious memories. Your experiments will no doubt familiarize you with the course of these displacements rather quickly. When will you go, my dear friend?"

St. Menoux stopped short, not knowing what to answer. He felt the cowardly soul of a guinea pig rise in him. The calm self-assurance of the invalid, instead of calming him, terrified him. The horror he had felt at the account on the radio rose again and overwhelmed him. In all truth, his life did not matter any more to the scientist than the life of the last coolie. To what terrifying unknown was he committing himself?

He thought he saw in Essaillon's eyes an avarice which terrified him and which, because of his silence, seemed to be growing little by little into a menace.

He turned around, considering the diving suit spread out on the pink marble. In an offhand manner which suited him poorly, he pinched the fabric of a sleeve, feeling it like a tailor. "Not today," he said sharply, "No, positively not today. I ate too much and especially drank too much. I don't feel master of myself. I would probably see the future with double vision."

He began to laugh, relieved at having got himself off the hook with a joke.

Excusing himself from his hosts, he strode off into the snow. In the cold, fresh air he breathed a sigh of joy like a drowning man who had just been revived.

3

St. Menoux had hardly got inside his door when remorse overtook him. Why should he be afraid when Annette, that child, had fearlessly offered herself to the experiments. If there was some danger, wasn't it worth a risk to undertake this stupendous adventure?

He reproached himself for having mistrusted his host. It was normal that Essaillon should appear impatient to know, normal also that he undertook the difficult experiments without emotion. The prodigious task which he had set for himself was justification enough.

Peter blamed the alcohol for his mistrust of the scientist and his fear of the moment of action. He slept soundly, waking up before dawn, sneezing in the freezing room.

He went down to the Bourgnat bar and was happy to find Mr. Michelet there, who helped him to kill time with a new account of his misadventures. The architect, delighted, led him to the other side of the boulevard, to the foot of his masterpiece, pointing out its virtues in detail.

The roof was sheathed with tiles glazed in different colors and arranged in a mosaic which showed a cat playing, one paw in the air. Eight black chimneys were topped by china animals—a sparrow as large as a turkey, a bull of the same stature, a bulldog, a pigeon, a rooster, a peacock and a carp. At the four corners of the building were bell towers, each one topped with a copper ball. Some figures sculpted in the round decorated the facade. A stag hunt was depicted at the level of the second floor. There was a pointed

45

window between the stag and the pack. A row of hunting horns supported the overhanging roof.

"It's more modern than acanthus leaves, at least," said Mr. Michelet.

This innovator had only given into tradition for the ornament over the entrance door, three classical heads of Medusa. He had begun a speech on the grace and nobility of the two steps that led to said door when nine o'clock sounded from a nearby bell tower. St. Menoux suddenly deserted the architect.

A half hour later, he rang the bell at No. 7 Racine Street and declared himself ready to begin the experiments.

At 10:30 A.M. standing in the middle of the laboratory, he buckled on the last strap of the knapsack. Annette, looking somewhat anguished, checked out all of his equipment. Tall and thin, clothed in his green attire, he resembled a tree trunk covered with moss. Through his glasses he saw Essaillon signal "Go." He pushed the depature button.

At the moment he pushed, he sneezed. His finger slipped on the button, putting only a little pressure on it. It seemed to him that his eyes and ears detached from his face, as well as his tongue, whose heat fled before him. His nose, swollen from a cold, broke off from his head like a loose tooth. He felt extraordinarily relieved. His feet no longer carried his weight. His body was as light as dust. His head was a bubble.

He felt himself become porous, invaded by a devouring penetration. This was his last impression. Even the weight of thought left him.

During the experiments in which Annette had participated, Essaillon had seen his daughter disappear suddenly, leaving the world without a transition. So he guessed that something irregular had happened when before his eyes, St. Menoux appeared as a phantom, the outline of his own form. A vertical force stretched this phantom upward, twisted it spirally, shaking him, trying to tear him from the floor where his feet were planted. Each second, he became more tenuous, more transparent.

"Quick!" shouted the scientist. "Annette, lamp 8!"

The young girl rushed to a switch. An enormous tube was lit on the ceiling. A blinding light enveloped the room, pushed aside the clarity of the day, pursued it outside the windows, burned the snow, made the trees snap, invaded the gardens, submerged houses, reached the entire quarter and climbed to the apex of the sky. Passersby raised their heads, stopping a second and shrugging their shoulders. "It's still this filthy war!" Nothing astonished them anymore. The next day the newspapers pointed it out as the aurora borealis and Abby Moreux made a statement about sunspots.

In the laboratory, everything grew incandescent. In a few seconds St. Menoux's phantom had shortened, contracted and solidified. The young teacher stood solid before the invalid. He finished sneezing. Essaillon held out an earnest hand, pushing on the return button of the apparatus.

"Close!" he shouted to his daughter.

The red light left the clouds, the streets and the roofs, reentered through the windows, and was reabsorbed in the tube, which then went out.

"Well, you see, I did not change place," said St. Menoux through the material of the diving suit.

"Nor time, my dear friend," answered Essaillon.

"Ah, I thought that I had arrived."

"No, you didn't leave."

The young man opened the hood. His face showed disappointment. By examining the apparatus and combining Annette's memories with St. Menoux's impressions, the scientist got a clue to what had happened.

"It's fascinating!" he said. "You didn't push the button down to the bottom. You received a very weak impulse and left your time without being able to reach another. You remained wedged between the present and the future. In short, you were in the conditional!"

He struck the arm of his chair and laughed like a child.

His beard rippled like a golden tide. St. Menoux began to understand the danger he had narrowly escaped. He did not find it very funny. He didn't feel fear however, but a purely intellectual consternation. His body recalled with delight his exquisite departure, the ethereal explosion of his senses. He could not resist a desire to begin again immediately. He closed the hood, adjusted his glasses, waved good-bye to his hosts and this time pushed down firmly on the button.

He almost fell. His foot struck a step. He saw nothing there. He recalled that he had adjusted his apparatus for a voyage into the future by only a half day. The scientist had advised him not to go too far for the first time and to set his arrival at night, in order to easily pass undetected.

The obscurity which surrounded him convinced him that he had arrived. He was astonished at the ease of his passage from the present to the future. He had felt nothing. If the apparatus was functioning properly, it should be around eleven o'clock in the evening. But where?

He took off his glasses in order to see more clearly. A vague odor struck his nostrils—an odor that seemed familiar. It smelled both like floor polish and the water closet, with a mild base of burned cauliflower. Taking a guess, he extended his hand and recognized the wooden banister. He was on the stairway of his hotel.

He began to laugh in the dark. He wanted to shout "fire" to wake up the whole house. His decent, middle-class reflexes restrained him. He was, however, too happy over the success of the experiment to let it pass. He was as delighted as a child with a new toy. He was, in any case, as naive and simple as a child in many ways. The solitary company of mathematics matures neither the heart nor the character. He decided to play a joke on Mr. Michelet. He would pass through the door, tickle his feet and pull on his beard. What a great idea!

He began climbing the stairs when suddenly the corridor light went on. Someone was coming. He put his finger on the

button of the vibrator, but remembered in time that he had
taken off his glasses. While he adjusted them, his hands
trembling in haste, the hall door opened and St. Menoux saw
climbing toward him, taking the steps two at a time—St.
Menoux.

It took his breath away. The other himself, the one who
was arriving, clothed as usual, smiled at him, pleased over his
astonishment. The meeting did not surprise him. He already
knew it. He was older by twelve hours. The two St.
Menouxs found themselves standing face to face on the
narrow landing. The lamp of the time switch lit them with
a yellow light. St. Menoux in the diving suit was filled with
emotion. His heart was beating with great thumps. He looked
at himself avidly. He removed his glasses and then his gloves.

St. Menoux in the overcoat watched with a delighted smile
as he went through the motions that he already knew. He
submitted willingly to the examination, turning around in
order to show himself from every angle. St. Menoux in the
diving suit finally caught his breath.

"It's—it's you," he said.

"You should say 'It's me!' replied the other, giving him
a poke in the ribs. St. Menoux in the diving suit smiled,
returning the punch. They both began to laugh, first softly,
then howling and gasping, clapping each other on the shoulders. Their peals of merriment filled the house. The corridor
light went out. They climbed the stairs they knew so well, arm
in arm in the darkness, still hiccuping with laughter. The
walls around them resounded from their footsteps.

When they were seated side by side on the edge of the
bed, their hands placed on their thin knees in the same
manner, he noticed that he felt an extreme happiness, a warm
glow and a feeling of security. Perhaps he had known similar
joy during his childhood, when, out of breath from playing,
he went to look for peace in his mother's arms. Since then
he had never met a being worthy of a similar trust. Suddenly,
he had found the perfect companion, the one men search for
in vain, the twin soul. Between them there were no lies, no

false reserve. Their egoism was exactly what they shared the best.

He hugged himself. It was strange to feel his four arms, his two living bodies. As the weather was cold, they undressed and slipped into the narrow bed, which their double presence soon heated. He didn't try to speak. What good would it do, since he knew everything about himself. Each man only seeks himself, in other men and women. He had found himself.

The power of their joy kept them from sleep. They would have liked never to leave one another. But the time of their meeting was not to exceed the twelve hours which subdivided St. Menoux. Otherwise, the second himself would disappear.

They got up around nine in the morning. He had a moment of anguish when he had to determine which one of the two was going to put on the diving suit. He was confused. Finally he smiled. Placing his hand on his stomach, he held out the other one toward his double.

"It's you," he said. "I remember that I ate last night at Essaillon's house. There was venison and wine. I didn't digest it very well."

Essaillon wiped his mouth and asked, "Do you understand why you arrived in your hotel's stairway?"

"Gosh no!" answered St. Menoux, who was attacking the venison and wine stew. "I didn't ask myself the question."

"I suppose you hadn't fixed your thought on anything. It was your body that decided. It had the habit of climbing or descending these stairs several times a day, automatically, without your mind paying the slightest attention to your legs. Your mind being uncommitted at the time of your departure, your body responded to a familiar movement and led you there."

"That's very possible," said St. Menoux. "Tomorrow I will try to govern myself better." Distracted, he was now in a hurry to leave.

The meal finished, he kissed Annette's hand, shook the fleshy hand of the scientist and headed home. The trip in the subway seemed endless to him. Once out of the station, he rushed toward his hotel, running in the dark up to the end of the hall, switching on the hall light and pushing open the glass door. He looked up.

Ten steps from him, St. Menoux, clothed in green, bewildered, watched him ascend the stairs.

For the second time, Peter relived this night of meeting himself. When his double returned to the past, he went back to Essaillon's villa. Leaving himself was heartbreaking. But he would find himself again when he wished. He carried the memory of his regret within him. He had only left himself in order to identify with himself better. He dreamed of a suit which would allow him to meet himself, not only with two St. Menouxs but with three, perhaps more. He saw himself as a group, a crowd, a multitude. He peopled the earth with himself alone. What an empathy! That must be Paradise. All the chosen ones in God's midst forming a single being.

"Can't you move over, you beanpole?"

A fat old woman in a black pleated skirt pushed him with her belly and her breasts. A man holding a briefcase under his arm drove an elbow into his ribs. A woman's green hood tickled his neck. He felt the head of a child against his rear. The subway was as full as a sardine can. Twenty-seven more people pushed in. The transit employees crammed the last ones in with blows on their backsides.

After consultation with the scientist, St. Menoux decided to make a more important jump into the future on this day. He arranged the markings on the index for a journey of one month and a supplementary half day to arrive at night. It was noon when he was ready to leave.

"Remember what I told you last night," advised Essaillon. "If you don't want to arrive just anywhere, try to fix your thought on something."

"That's easy," answered St. Menoux. He placed his finger

on the departure button and wondered what to think of. Nothing interested him particularly. The first image which came to his mind was the Place de la Concorde. As he was going to press the button, he noticed that his mind was already very far from the Place. He focused on the image of the streets. They reminded him of a graphic solution to a problem, of the paper on which he had designed it, of the merchant who had sold him the paper, of the movie theater next to the stationery shop and of Tino Rossi's face on the billboards. He caught himself humming "Veni, veni, veni . . ."

His mind came back to the Place de la Concorde. The horse carriages reminded him of fragrant manure piles. This succession of images unfolded in his mind at a frightening speed.

He brought his mind back a third time to the Square where the Obelisk stands. The Obelisk reminded him of the Pyramids, the Pyramids of Napoleon, Napoleon of Josephine, Josephine of a hammock, a hammock of a sailor, a sailor of the sea, the sea of oysters, the oysters of a lemon.

Furious, he pressed the button, no longer knowing what he was thinking.

A chandelier, very faintly lit and colored in green by his glasses, was hanging from a ceiling above him. He was in bed. A woman's perfume filtered muskily to his nostrils through his hood. Light blankets covered his body; an arm, scarcely heavier, was laying across his chest. He slowly turned his head. Annette was asleep against him.

She was lying on her side, her face calm in sleep, her breathing slow. Two brown locks traced an arabesque on the embroidered sheet. Her languid body touched Peter's. He felt the round softnesses of it, her breast slowly rising against his right arm, her thigh against his thigh. She slept peacefully, abandoned and confident. The closed door protected her and the night light chased away gloomy dreams. With his large bones and his rough garments, he had planted himself like a thorn in the tender body of this virgin night.

He felt, through all of his clothes, the warmth, the roundness and the tender weight of this neighboring body penetrate his body, rounding it, garnishing it with softness and
volume. His heart was beating fast. He realized that he loved
Annette. He had been too preoccupied to notice it sooner.
Normally he was aloof to loving, except the infinite com-
binations of numbers and abstract figures which delighted his
mind. Since he had met Essaillon, he had felt that passion
which stifles all others for those whom it arouses: scientific
curiosity. His love for Annette had been born within him
without his noticing it. That is how he had come through
time and space to the place where he hoped to find satisfaction. Peter reflected that his body had behaved like a
pirate. Yet the happiness that flooded him chased away his
fear.

It was different than the egotistical and sterile joy of the
preceding night—a feeling of incomparable physical well-
being, of gold in his veins, of sunshine in his chest. A sun
—yes, he felt as glorious as the sun on the harvest. A crazy
desire mounted in him to take Annette softly and tenderly
into his arms. Annette, rounded and soft as a fruit, abandoned
close to him. Yet if he moved, she would wake and cry out
in terror.

The force of his love swells his muscles, accelerates his
blood, making his temples spin. His ears are burning—he
guesses they must be bright red. His burning hands are
sweating in his gloves. He doesn't dare flutter an eyelash. He
is bewildered with joy and shame. He loves. A cramp gnaws
at his groin. The young girl's perfume pierces him. His
torture equals his bliss. He thinks also that it is unseemly to
enter a loved woman's bed with his boots on.

Annette is dreaming. She is at the seashore. A tower of
white marble rises among the waves. The fine lacework of a
spiral stairway twines around her up toward the clouds.
"Above all, don't forget the three ounces of mercury flower,"
says her father. The golden waves of the scientist's beard
caress the bottom of the tower. A procession of children is

climbing the stairway. The three ounces are above her at
the summit. Peter is descending in a parachute, a gun in
hand. "Peter. . ." she sighs. She half awakes, opens her eyes.
Peter moves under her hand. She stretches, spreading her
arms and legs. Her entire body is content; she falls again
into sleep.

At Annette's sigh, St. Menoux had pressed the button of the
vibrator, which he had not used during his first voyage. The
visible world was immediately transformed. The round globe
of the night light became parabolic, the bed doubled in size
and Annette's face lengthened as in a mirror. Peter made
the necessary movements to get up. But instead of standing,
he passed through the bed, found himself under the cross
beam, slipped to the side, and was immobilized.

He had the impression that he was sitting in the middle of
the bedroom. Before him, where legs should have been, there
was only transparent air. In anguish he touched himself. He
felt hard and present. Yet when he put his hand in front of his
eyes, nothing hid the half-open drawer of the commode from
his gaze. He suddenly realized what it was—he no longer saw
himself. Essaillon had forgotten to warn him. He himself
should have guessed it. The glasses would show him the time
in which he had not yet found himself. They could not trans-
mit his image to him.

When he tried to get up and walk, he sank halfway into
the floor, then ascended slowly to the ceiling, in which his
head disappeared. He did not weigh on this world which was
not his. Only his muscular impetus projected him to the
right, to the left, upwards, downwards, without his being able
to gain support on anything. Peter struggled for a long time
before he succeeded in controlling himself. When he raised
his foot to walk, the spring of his leg drew it upward and he
began to turn around like the arms of a windmill under a
light breeze. He reassembled his limbs, unbent and left like a
frog jumping over a wall.

He got used little by little to his new way of moving

around and to the strange sensation of possessing a solid
warm body which his hands felt, but which did not exist in
his eyes. He almost succeeded in going where he wanted. He
threw one limb ahead, letting himself be propelled by the
spring which nothing braked. A gesture of his arm drew him
through phantom houses.

At the first gesture which carried him away, he was relieved to find the night again. He did not see himself, but
he didn't see anything else either. He was no different from
any venturing Parisian without a flashlight in the blackout.
Except that he no longer risked a fall or a bump. The night
did not bring him any surprises and could not place any
obstacle in his path. The material world had lost all substance for him.

When he looked at the light, he had the impression, since
the vibrator changed the appearance of things, of wandering
among the images of a film projected by a strange lantern.

He could begin to look around him. In the transparent
beds he saw entwined couples struggling. He entered a tiny
basement nightclub through the ceiling. Its walls were covered with mirrors, to make it look bigger. He descended to
the middle of a table and stopped. His left foot was in the
champagne bucket and his right hand hung in the congested
head of a drinker. The mouth of a drunken girl, who was
roaring with laughter, was exactly placed in his groin. He
stood erect, invisible and solid in the middle of a visible and
soft universe.

Glimpsing a strange object in the mirror, he looked again,
recognizing with bewilderment, two steps away from him,
two eyes without a face. They were the size of fried eggs, two
round eyes with eyebrows and the beginning of cheeks.

He approached the mirrored wall slowly. Slowly the eyes
grew larger, suspended in space like two moonfish in an
aquarium. A shiver ran down St. Menoux's back. A thousand
fears disturbed his rational mind. Were these eyes the horrible
trace of a spectre, of a demon, which his apparatus rendered
visible to his mortal eyes? For how long would they wander

in space, at the quest of what paradise, what purgatory, condemned to which awful punishment?

St. Menoux felt a chill of horror. He had just penetrated the great mystery of a kingdom which is not of this world. The eyes stared out, immobile, at the height of his face. He nearly cried out. The living beings who stirred around him were incapable of seeing him, but these phantom eyeballs saw him, looked into his eyes with an expression of indescribable astonishment and disgust.

Was he so ugly, so pitiful? He felt himself pierced to the core of his miserable soul by this gaze. He rediscovered the overpowering fear which had choked him as a child when he had to make his first confession. Tears came to his eyes. He saw two identical ones shine in the floating eyeballs. Suddenly he burst out laughing. Now he understood. He winked his left eye. Opposite, the right eye closed. He sniffled and called himself an idiot. They were his own eyes reflected in the mirror. His eyes, the only part of his body which he could see because their image passed through the glasses in both directions!

He breathed a deep sigh. He found his equilibrium again. No mystery. What was he searching for? There was only science. He was happy to see even this little of himself. The round eyes smiled.

He had almost forgotten the place where he had found himself. He looked around again. The pale faces multiplied in the mirrors, waving like seedpods agitated by the wind. The lights went out. A naked singer undulated in the beam of a spotlight. She was crying words which mingled with one another. Her navel looked as large as a mouth. In the stirring shadows, the crowd of diners was leering and gorging itself.

St. Menoux went away slowly, crossing through the beam of light without breaking it, then through the mirror, a china cabinet, the dirty dishwater, a roof, an obscure cellar, yards of ground and cement. He found himself on the quay of a closed subway station. He went down an empty gallery, lit by two naked light bulbs. A train passed by on the track.

Five hundred compressed persons rushed on in this desert world. A rat, bigger than a pig, disappeared into a pinhole.

In a moment St. Menoux left the underground, climbed up to the top of a bourgeois house and saw, as he passed by, a drunken woman counting her spoons and sleeping between two hams. Her husband left the neighboring bedroom on tiptoes to find the maid in curlers. He paid her with a piece of cold veal. The traveler continued his walk.

He slipped through space, sometimes with his feet in the air, at other times flat on his stomach, wound into a ball or stretched out like a gliding bird. He slid headfirst into triple-locked bedrooms, discovering men in their moment of abandon and open betrayal. Men and women alone and marriages which for years had hid nothing were exposed before this invisible witness.

Perhaps the vibrator revealed them uglier than they were in truth—deformed, wretched, swollen and discolored. Little by little St. Menoux forgot his glasses and no longer made any difference between his vision and the real. He saw the gray lingerie come off the gray skins, laying bare thin, twisted thighs, swollen stomachs with distended navels. Black scales marbled the feet. Enormous breasts floated like bloated fish in the Seine. Others, flat, hung to the ground. Toenails entangled under beds, bony arms spread out and folded again, menacing the walls with their elbows. Greenish heads of hair spread on the pillows of the slimy beds and hanging hands scratched forests of hair and touched withered sex organs. Before going to bed, the grocer in the back of his store watered down the wine and stole two large coffee beans and three cubes of sugar from each pound of rations.

Peter moved to the other end of the city. He sprang from one wall to another, across the moonless streets, letting himself be carried away by these jumps through lighted and obscure rooms. In apartments with wool rugs and silk curtains, he saw phantoms in satin dressing gowns leave their beauty before the mirror and go to bed with their stomachs in folds and mud packs on their faces. In large brick barracks

where the poor huddled, weary mothers counted potatoes
and cut bread in transparent slices for the next day.

At the homes of the bourgeois and the miserable, he
found the same immense fatigue. Men and women, with
the same weary gesture, turned out the last lamp and
stretched out in the night.

The resignation to making a living, to richness, to misery,
to lost days, to too-short time, to vague hopes, to wives, to
husbands, to bosses, to pleasures, to pain, weighed down
upon these millions of stretched-out bodies, snoring, gnashing,
groaning, shriveling and stretching in grotesque poses without
finding a second's peace.

Peter had forgotten Annette's soft bedroom as he discovered
humanity. He was impassioned by thus viewing men, his
brothers. Sometimes he found in the filth of a tenement or
in the luxurious coldness of a rich man's crib, the peaceful
countenance of a child. He lingered over this miracle, wondering how such a beautiful promise could end in such
futility.

A few children were disfigured by the vibrator. Some
already showed signs of their father's vices. Yet the majority
of them seemed like new beings. To remain a child, was
this the secret? St. Menoux understood the enormity of the
task which he had undertaken in Essaillon's company. He
doubted his ability to do anything for mankind.

He crossed a hospital room and sniffed. He smelled nothing. From the time he pressed the triangular button, he had
been cut off from the odors of the world. He scarcely paid
attention, normally, to olfactory sensations. The absence of
odors reminded him of their existence in the same way an
unsalted meal recalls the presence of salt in foods where it
is only slightly tasted.

The slum where six persons were sleeping, the street swept
by the night wind, the deserted public urinal where
constrained water was singing, and the abandoned slip of the
coquette woman—all left no odor for him. Nor this room
full of the noise of suffering beings which he passed through

in flying steps. The vibrator soldered the beds together into a large platform. The sad glow of the night light illumined a display of cut limbs and volcanic abscesses. Wound bandages strangled the life out of victims and balls of cotton stifled their last breaths. Through the bandages came muffled cries, waves of groaning and death rattles of dawn. These wounded and decayed beings who fought against evil and medicine, who shouted to frighten death away, and who should have smelled of ether and carrion, were as odorless as a nightmare.

In a glass room, the hospital attendant on guard was sleeping, collapsed in a white heap in a chair, a hypodermic needle in his hand and a smile under his moustache.

St. Menoux, dreadfully weary, judged that he had seen enough. He re-entered the street. In the middle of the pavement he stopped the vibrator, falling on his rear. The cold night slammed against him. From the mouth of a sewer rose a warm vapor. Joyfully he inhaled its stench. He got up, rubbing his behind. The frost cracked under his feet. The wind had swept away the clouds. Houses vaguely lit by the stars reacquired their opaque mass.

St. Menoux placed his hand on a lamp post, topped with a chlorotic bulb. Through his glove he felt the icy solid cast iron. The meager light lit his boots, his green thighs, his stomach, and his chest with the glittering zipper. He smiled at his rediscovered body, raising his hands. With his fingers spread out, he made little puppets before his delighted eyes. Some steps grated on the frozen ground. Three yards away two policemen appeared. Peter burst out laughing. Indignation stopped the policemen short. To laugh during the curfew! They whistled and marched toward him, but found only the wind.

St. Menoux did not tell Essaillon and his daughter about his intrusion into her bed. He related his voyage through the city and complained about the deformities the glasses and earphones imposed on the world and its noises. He had a migraine which swelled his eyes. He still had a humming in his ears. He took a sleeping pill and was out for ten hours. When he woke up, he felt relieved and could draw a conclusion from the experiment.

"We are attempting the impossible," he said to the scientist. "Certainly, nothing can be done to pull men from their misery."

"Let's understand each other," interrupted Essaillon impatiently. "I do not claim to reform men and to remove from each the sufferings that he creates for himself. But we may be able to remove from all men some great collective misfortunes. We shall do what we can. We are not God, after all."

St. Menoux asked only to be convinced. It was the end of the meal. While closing his eyes in pleasure, Essaillon emptied a large glass of brandy. Peter drank a gulp, choked, coughed and turned purple.

"To know! To know! That is our first duty!" exclaimed the invalid lyrically. "You shall soon have new glasses and perfected earphones. So taste this liqueur. A marvel! It will perhaps be more mild to your throat. It is necessary to continue the experiments, to completely familiarize yourself with the apparatus and soon to plunge far into the future. I am anxious to know what will be the destiny of the great-grandchildren of our great-grandchildren."

St. Menoux, suddenly very serious, looked at the scientist opposite him. He had never appeared so large. His stomach truly began at his shoulders, raising his beard almost horizontally. The light of the window lit Essaillon from behind, revealing a small fringe of transparent down on the top of his skull. Below it his ears spread out slightly, round, well-hemmed and plump, rising above the flow of the beard like luminous shells.

Annette was seated on Peter's right. He hardly dared to turn his glance toward her. He recalled more the shame than the happiness he had felt in her bed. He would have liked to forget the whole incident and not create some misfortune for himself. How could this young girl, so beautiful and fresh, love him? He knew that he did not possess enough flesh on his bones, that his small, clear eyes with their colorless eyelashes, and his oak-colored hair, flat and dull, which persisted in falling in oblique locks on his forehead, offered nothing seductive. He also knew that his complexion evoked illness more than joy and that he was somewhat twisted and ridiculously tall. He would have liked to lower his head by ten inches. Annette scarcely came up to his breastbone.

He went to the laboratory, hobbling slightly. The boots had heated his feet, giving him a blister. Annette pushed her father, who was winded by the meal. While Peter was slipping on the diving suit, she looked at him with a frankness which nothing disturbed. If he had been less naive and more sure of himself, he would have drawn joy from these looks.

Annette didn't read novels. She had perhaps never seen the word "love" written. Educated by her father, she had already pushed her study of sciences very far at an age when most children are still playing, and with the same pleasure. The laboratory had replaced fairy tales. The reality of the world did not seem so solid to her. She had seen too many things transformed between her father's magical fingers, time stretching or contracting, and the form of her life disappearing, returning, changing. The extraordinary was her normal domain.

This daily wonder had preserved in her mind a childlike freshness while her heart and body were blooming. The scientist had not wasted time teaching her the rules of life. Reaching her spring, she did not try to submerge the desires that rose naturally within her.

The night of Tremplin-le-Haut had seen a third person enter this astonishing universe that she shared with her father —a clumsy, dirty man, disguised as a soldier. She guessed instinctively that he was full of kindness and gentleness. During the two years she was separated from him, she did not stop thinking of this profound man with the sallow face who shared her mysteries. She waited impatiently to see him again. Her father had not noticed that she had grown.

The laugh with which she had welcomed St. Menoux was
a laugh of joy. He had not guessed. He had been too
captivated by the scientist's words.

Without being able to say exactly to herself what she was
waiting for, she knew what would happen. Perhaps he would
take her in his arms. She did not try to immagine the words
he would say. He would use awkward gestures. She was
content, for the time being, with the happiness of waiting. He
would finish by opening his eyes, by seeing her near him . . .

"What is necessary, my young Peter," said Essaillon, "is to
learn to control yourself. Know where you are going. Are
you ready? Go to it!"

St. Menoux had been carried away the first time by his
legs, the second time by his heart. For the third experiment,
he wanted his head to lead him. He strained to forget his
body and his feelings, to be no more than a thinking being.
His head, his head alone! He had the impression of facing
nothingness.

He left while jumping from the total absence of voluntary
thought to the dizzy unfolding of absolutely strange asso-
ciations of thought.

At first glance, he recognized the place of his arrival.
Forty faces were looking at him stupefied, the faces of forty
adolescents with fuzzy hair and acne. He was standing in
front of the blackboard in his mathematics class at the Philip-
August high school. His own class where he had not been
since he went into the Army.

At eighteen nothing is astonishing. The green phantom
who had just appeared resembled strongly—with his height,
his large head, his round back, and his gaunt torso—the
caricature of the disappeared teacher which Alberes had
drawn in his spare time and which had become so popular.
After the first surprise, there was delirium. The boys slammed
the lids of their desks, then began to sing: "The phantom
with us! The phantom with us!"

The new teacher, a young, timid temporary, tried to re-establish order with a "shush, shush!" which no one heard. Alberes, the stocky Southerner, climbed on his desk and began a speech, exaggerating his "r's". An eraser shut his mouth. The teacher leaped up, opening the door and went to look for help. Books and notebooks flew across the classroom. Jumping over obstacles, the forty students rushed toward the apparition which a gemometry textbook had just hit on the head.

Peter just had time to switch on the vibrator. The book flew by him and fell on the floor with a dull noise followed by a disappointed groan. The door opened suddenly. A procession of shadows crawled up to the front of the class. In spite of the distortion, St. Menoux recognized the headmaster, the assistant headmaster, the superintendent, the bursar and the caretaker, followed by the temporary teacher. The teacher was trembling so much that his contours were blurred.

Upon the arrival of the older men, the students calmed down and took their places. St. Menoux was surprised at his disappointment over this show of good behavior. He felt himself becoming a schoolboy again. The same urge to play which had seized him on his first experiment arose again in him. He stole to the teacher's chair and stopped the vibrator.

A frenzy overwhelmed the class when the boys saw the green phantom lean over, pick up the assistant headmaster's toupee, erase the figures traced on the blackboard with it and write in large letters: "Vive la liberté!" After which he crossed his arms on his chest and vanished.

The forty adolescents turned over their desks, roaring with joy, surrounded the authorities and fell on them, undressing them and throwing their clothes out the window.

The phantom appeared in the doorway and made a sign: "Come." The torrent rushed on. Young and old abandoned the fears of punishment, the anguish of examinations and aimed at the partitions, pulverizing the inner walls. The high school was no more than an immense vessel boiling with

the furious joy of ten thousand students who had just rediscovered their youth. The headmaster, without a stitch, led
the dance. The roof flew off, the walls trembled and fell.
Joy ran through the town. It was the first day of spring.

Essaillon was thoughtful on hearing St. Menoux's new
account.

"You aren't serious enough," he reproached Peter. "The
diving suit must be an instrument of research for you, not
a toy or a means of upsetting the lives of others. Certainly you
will have to intervene in the lives of some men. Isn't that
our essential goal? But you must seek to make them happy,
not to amuse them. It is not the same thing at all."

The little flame of gaiety that Peter saw dancing in
Annette's eyes destroyed the entire effect of her father's
sermon. He was not, however, satisfied. Again he had left
without knowing where he was going. This time it was his
head that had drawn him. It had led him to the very place
where it was used to working. But his will had not intervened.

He tried new experiments without any more success. They
brought him to the secret reserves of a chocolate maker
where his sweet tooth led him, twice again into Annette's
bed, happily empty, and to the toilet, where the urge to
relieve himself led him.

"It seems useless to me," he said to Essaillon, "to continue
my excursions into the immediate future any longer. My
habits and my needs transport me to my time and to neighboring time. Perhaps I shall be able to liberate myself from
it if I jump bluntly one hundred years ahead. Tomorrow I
shall go to the year 2042."

"No . . . no . . ." said the scientist a bit hesitatingly. "Not
2042, but 2052."

His pink skull had blushed and his ears were glowing.

"Why these ten years more?" asked St. Menoux, surprised.

"Here is why." The obese man had recovered his assur-
ance. He probed his beard and drew out a small book from
his inner vest pocket. Worn gilt letters decorated the leather

cover marbled with spots of old age. Peter leaned over the volume. Essaillon had opened it to page 113 and pointed out a verse to him.

"These are the prophecies of Nostradamus. Read this poem!"

St. Menoux read:

> The year that Venus is closest to Mars
> Aquarius' tap is turned off
> The large house will have fallen in flame
> The dying cock will leave man naked.

" 'The year that Venus is closest to Mars' astrologically means the year 2052," said the scientist. "The other lines prophesy some terrible events. The cock designates here, France—or perhaps humanity.

" 'Will leave man naked' . . . Man naked! Do you understand? What could happen to our unfortunate grandsons? Don't you wish to know?"

St. Menoux did not dare express his astonishment. How could this man of genius take such gibberish so seriously?

"The prophecy of Saint Olive concurs with this," the invalid went on. "In the year 2052, the river of war and peace must begin again to flow and stop at the same hour. The saint adds that thereafter it will no longer flow. Could this be the universal peace?"

"Hum," said the young professor, "that seems quite improbable to me!"

4

Peter was astonished to arrive in the year 2052 at the foot of the Sacré-Coeur Church. He was at the base of the stairs. Before him, the familiar cupolas raised their unaltered silhouettes. Their color had darkened. The white stone had taken the dirty tinge that covers all the monuments of Paris. St. Menoux turned around to glance at the great city. Paris had disappeared.

In its place a stupefied Peter saw a field of flat cement. Here and there rose a few buildings of little importance and a great number of oval-shaped objects, the height of a three-story house, built of a colored transparent matter. Around each of these enormous eggs coiled the spirals of a kind of gigantic screw. Some remained standing, like the egg of Christopher Columbus, but most of them were turned over and several of them were broken. What seemed strangest to St. Menoux was the absence of life. He did not see a living being.

His finger on the button of the vibrator, ready to disappear, he advanced toward the closest of these objects. A powerful warm wind pushed against him. He had to stoop over to walk. He began to perspire. The sun emitted a tropical heat. St. Menoux drew near the gigantic egg. It was laying on its side, split open. It seemed to have fallen from the the sky. An intuition came to him. He was standing on an airfield and these ovoids surrounded by a helix were the new airplanes. But what catastrophe could have provoked the fall of all those that lay in debris before him?

Through the transparent shell he saw several people inside

the plane, clothed in brightly colored overalls, stretched out
and fastened to the debris of the plane in abandoned attitudes of death. An odor of decay escaped from the crevices
of the machine. St. Menoux, choking, overcome by emotion,
hurried to get away. Had he come so far into the future only
to meet corpses? A silence disturbed only by the wind's
whistling rage reigned in this sunburned area. Peter was burning up in his winter clothes and his wool diving suit. He
decided to leave the plain of scorching cement. He took off
his glasses, squinting his eyes under the dazzling light. When
he could see better, he looked around and saw that the
aerodrome was surrounded by a kind of railing of tall glass
pillars. After ten minutes of walking, he reached their pe-
riphery. He crossed the last yards running, pushing his head
between two pillars where he was seized with dizziness. He
was in the open sky.

Very low, below him, stretched the infinite sea of Parisian
roofs, the same gray sea that he remembered seeing from
the top of the Eiffel Tower. The capital had barely changed
in a century. A few long rectilinear avenues crossed the
crowds of tiny houses. To the west, to the south, to the east,
rose three skyscrapers next to which those of twentieth
century New York would have seemed puny. St. Menoux
concluded that he himself was on the roof top of a similar
building, built on the Montmartre hill. The architects had
preserved the Sacré-Coeur by perching it on the very top of
the immense building.

St. Menoux aimed his telescope toward the capital lying at
his feet. What he saw was proof that an extraordinary
catastrophe had occurred. Files of immobile automobiles
covered the avenues. Small boats, barges and tugs along the
Seine were heaped up by the current against the piers of the
bridges. Planes had fallen on the city and had smashed the
roofs, ripping open the houses.

In the darkest streets, sheltered from the sun, St. Menoux
finally saw some men moving, clothed in the same overalls
as the dead occupants in the plane. He looked for women's

skirts, concluding finally that they were dressed like the men. These costumes vaguely resembled his diving suit. He thought that he could mingle in the crowd without attracting too much attention.

With a movie camera furnished with a telephoto lens, he took several views of Paris. He returned to film close up an airplane intact, the debris of another, the details of a dead's person's clothes and a panoramic view of the roof.

As he was wondering how to find a way to get down, the wind carried to him the smell of smoke and the noise of an alarm bell. He went back to the edge of the terrace. Enormous flames rose from the lines of cars which covered the boulevards. The wind pushed the flames onto the houses which blazed by entire districts. The smoke already reached as high as he was. He pointed his camera at the conflagration which was now at the foot of the skyscraper. The thought of the unfortunate people who were being cooked in this furnace overwhelmed him. Whirlwinds of nauseous smoke filled the sky. Some sparks fell on him, threatening to burn his clothes. All of Paris was aflame. Half-suffocating, he readjusted his glasses and pressed the return button.

Essaillon, overcome with impatience, was waiting for him in the laboratory. Peter, still pale, related what he had seen. The invalid clenched his fat hands on the arms of his chair, pulling his beard.

"God, how I would have loved to be with you!" he murmured.

"I think I know why I arrived on the terrace of the skyscraper," said St. Menoux. "I left carried away by curiosity. It led me to a place where I could see everything."

"You didn't see everything. We must find out what happened. You are going to return there. Bring several films. You—"

"I'm tired," objected St. Menoux. "I want to eat and sleep. We will put the next trip off until tomorrow, if that's all right with you."

"Excuse me," said the obese man, sighing. "Of course you must rest."

For the rest of his voyages, St. Menoux used a method which he regretted not having thought of sooner. He got hold of photographs of the country and postcards of French cities and foreign nations. He looked at one of them at the time of each departure and filled his mind with its image. He thus was able to control himself. He traveled across the earth in every direction and knew that the terrible catastrophe extended throughout the world. America, Asia, Australia and Europe were all prey to the flames, famine and all other aspects of the plague. Men fled everywhere, surrounded by a thousand forms of death.

It took a long time for Peter to learn the origin of this catastrophe. Even in France he could not understand the conversations of the fugitives. Each time that he found a book or an abandoned newspaper, he discovered the same familiar French, slightly enriched with some new technical terms. But when he listened to spoken words, he had the impression of being abroad. The spoken language was totally different from the written word. Yet it seemed to him that he heard the same language in the middle of the city ruins along the Seine, or in the inflamed Russian Steppe, or in the mouths of the black South Americans.

Little by little, thanks to his knowledge of several European languages, and with the help of Essaillon to whom he brought back some phrases, he arrived at an idea about the new language.

Large movements of population, moving armies, exchanges of manpower, emigrations and massive deportations must have come about during the century. The national languages had interpenetrated and melted into one common language. This new language evolved around a simplified syntax from words borrowed from all the languages. Each one had furnished the vocabulary most proper to its genius: French, the terms of culinary art and love; German, technical words and those of philosophy and strategy; English, those of commerce, and Italian, the superlatives. The Slavic languages offered a complete choice of oaths rich in consonants.

The old words combined their phonetic essentials. Their evolution was made so quickly that the new European language could not be written. The same syllable pronounced almost in the same way by a Spaniard, a Frenchman, an Englishman, a Russian or a German was written by them in five very different ways.

Thus the old French persisted in its written form. Everyone knew his own national language, which tended to become, little by little, a dead language. The new means of world expression, which evolved and grew, constantly lost old cells and acquired new ones, like a living organism. The Asiatic languages alone seemed immune to this mixing.

One day St. Menoux understood how a civilization built on so many centuries of progress had been able to collapse in so little time, leaving the world to chaos and death. He told Essaillon about his discovery. Electricity had suddenly disappeared!

"You must believe," said the scientist, "that a premonition led me to renounce the use of electricity in the apparatus that you are wearing on your belt. Otherwise, once arrived in the year 2052, you would not have been able to return!"

St. Menoux shuddered. He saw himself abandoned in the middle of this world among the stopped motors, dead cities and naked men. He measured once more the dangers which he risked in his experiments, but never thought for a second of abandoning them.

He was in a hurry, like Essaillon, to know what was going to become of the men who would survive the cataclysm. Material progress did not seem to have brought them peace nor happiness. Would the world deprived of machines be happier? Yet how many would escape the catastrophe, and in which region of the world could they be found?

St. Menoux used a photograph of a crowd cut from a magazine. It showed thousands of men and women gathered together, massed out to the horizon, their heads raised, mouths open, dumbfounded and occupied, looking at something happening in the sky.

Peter did not doubt that the movement of this swarming of life would lead him toward the ones who had escaped.

He arrived in the middle of a curious gray fog, a dry fog which limited his view to a few yards. The sun, which burned like the mouth of a blast furnace, looked enormous to him, surrounded by a halo. A tree twisted its naked branches in the overheated air. A continuous noise, similar to the roaring of a waterfall, filled his ears. He almost lost his equilibrium. The ground had just given way under his feet.

Peter looked around. His boots were buried in the chest of a half-rotted corpse. A billion flies swarmed around him. He guessed in horror the nature of the haze. It was an immense swarm of flies which whirled and obscured the horizon. The innumerable buzzings were what he had thought to be a waterfall, and what was making the air tremble. A viscous stench boiled under the sun. Gagging, Peter pushed on the button of the vibrator. He found himself immediately closed in his little universe outside of time. He felt there only the warmth of his body, smelled only the camphorated odor of the noelite. But the memory of the stench stuck to his nostrils. It took him a few minutes to recover. The infernal heat now crossed through him without afflicting him.

A gust of wind swept away the last shriveled leaves that trembled at the top of the tree, hollowing whirlpools in the thickness of the insects, clearing the view up to the horizon for an instant. Peter saw himself in the center of a plain covered with dead bodies. On top of them swarmed a carpet of flies, a thick, glittering moving crust. The heavy wind stopped, the thick air closed around St. Menoux. The enormous roaring started up again.

The new accessories of the vibrator transmitted the images and noises without deforming them. Essaillon had added to

the new white glasses a system of prisms, which allowed Peter
to see himself as well as the exterior objects. The apparatus
was held to his head with four crossed straps. The perfected
earphones and viewfinders, whose weight had tripled, tired
him more than the preceding outfit.

He had not succeeded in curing his head cold, which was
turning into sinusitis. Several times since adolescence doctors
had advised him to have his adenoids removed as well as
his tonsils, and also to use the opportunity to get rid of his
appendix. But St. Menoux preferred to blow his nose.

Perhaps because of this head cold and in spite of the
temptation, he could not bear the vibrator for more than
an hour and a half without interruption. It was rare that he
had to use it for such a long time.

After a last glance around the area, he understood that
there was nothing for him to do in this place. He searched
for a living being. The image of the multitude had led him
to the multitude of the dead. He now had to return to the
laboratory and find another means of propelling himself toward the survivors.

He wiped his nose through the hood and prepared to stop
the vibrator before pressing the return button. But he stopped
his gesture in anguish. A swarm of flies had just crossed
through his hand.

The state in which he found himself, although rendering
the universe permeable to him, rendered him, in turn, permeable to everything. The first day he had tried the perfected glasses, he hadn't been able to walk through the walls
and furniture which seemed as solid as his body without some
apprehension. The first time that he had seen the arm of a
chair enter his chest, he'd felt the same emotional shock as
if he had been pierced by a spear. Then he became accustomed to separating his nervous reflexes from his visual sensations. He even took pleasure, after a while, in playing with
these appearances and in mingling, for example, with the
trunk of a tree, stretching out his arms among the branches

and seeing the flowered boughs come out of each one of his fingers.

But he had to be careful to find himself alone, without any object inside him, when he stopped the vibrator. It was not hard to imagine the damage to his organism if he should taken his normal place in time when he was around the back of a chair or even in a bouquet of flowers.

That is what made him interrupt his gesture. Flies were passing through his body. He saw them coming out, isolated or in bands, from his thighs, his belly and the palms of his hands. They were swarming in the place of his intestines and humming between his ears.

He absolutely had to get away from this place infested with insects before taking on his present state. If not, he would find himself stuffed with encysted little animals carried along by his blood. That would be instant death by poisoning or embolism if some hairy beast was found wrapped in the tender matter of the brain or an essential nerve.

He searched for some indication that would allow him to determine his course. But the horizon was obscured everywhere by the moving fog of insects through which the sun sometimes cast rainbows. He saw only the tragic gesture of the arid tree which the sky of iron was crushing into dust. He decided to go to the right. He went as fast as possible, rushing ahead on all fours rowing through a bit of air which did not contain its one hundred insects.

He bitterly regretted turning on the vibrator without thinking. But there was no time for regrets. He had to hurry. The plain went on indefinitely with its black horde of dead. Sometimes the horrible swarming of the insects was torn and he could see the bright color of a piece of clothing or a sneering face whose teeth or nose bone were broken. The air, stirred with billions of whirling wings, vibrated and grated like a concert of violins played by the insane. Peter, suffering from delusions, felt fatigue closing in on him. His migraine and fear began to beat at his temples. He forged straight

ahead and clouds of flies passed through him. A living
and buzzing hail filled the decayed atmosphere.

Suddenly an idea came to him. He could escape the insects
by moving vertically. He raised his arms as if he were at
prayer and rose with the gestures of an angel, his large limbs
weakly moving. He saw with indescribable joy that the flies
became rarer. Their buzzing was weaker and further away,
mingling with the throbbing of his migraine. He reached the
height of the clouds. He floated alone in the sky. Very low,
below him, the earth seemed veiled with a grey mist which
curled to the arc of the horizon. He put his finger on the
triangular button. For the second time, a kind of instinct
saved him. If he were to stop the vibrator now, he would fall
like a stone, crashing to the ground in a burst of insects
and decayed flesh. He must resume his voyage.

He looked again at the desolate earth. Very far ahead
it seemed to him that smoke was rising toward the sky.
He began again his flight, like a butterfly, a snowflake, a
seedpod or a grasshopper. His view was already cloudy.
Anguish gripped his heart. He was afraid of fainting, of not
recovering and of remaining forever wandering through the
blue sky like a derisive phantom in suspense above the
centuries until the apparatus, out of order one day, would let
his ashes fall in light puffs on a new civilization. He opened
his eyes wide, then closed them, squinting his eyelids in order
to find a clearer view for a few seconds. Below the smoke,
the ruins of an immense city appeared. The walls, blackened
by the fire, stretched out along the dry river as far as the
eye could see.

Peter regained hope. He descended softly, penetrating the
wall of insects and reaching the first houses. The flies were
rarer here, because the dead of this city had burned along
with it. The overwhelmed voyager finally found a corner in
the shade deserted by the horrible insects. He breathed a
deep sigh and pressed his hands to his temples. A hammer
was pounding at his skull with each heartbeat; his squinted
eyes made his eyesockets cramped.

Immobilized, he stopped breathing and listened. He heard his heart beating like a drum. The wail of a violin like a shrill tune rose from his belly to his head. A tiny fly, a shining drop of green gold, burst from his face, made three hesitating turns and re-entered his shoulder. He shook himself, stopping again; it was buzzing somewhere in his thigh. He jumped in the air, leaping and perching himself on a ruined wall. He heard the little music rising and descending, whirling in his chest. He plunged into masses of ashes and burned stones. As soon as he stopped again, he heard the infernal vibrato piercing his flesh and bones.

He was at the end of his rope. A stream of blood flowed in front of his eyes. He escaped toward the sky, making a desperate effort to look round again. A fire was still burning near the river. He gathered his last strength to go there. He reached it on his stomach. His head had grown like a pumpkin, like a balloon. There was the fire. He threw himself into it open-mouthed, rolling around in its flames, howling with joy, imagining the end of the horrible little beast who was crackling and shriveling in the purifying flame.

He stopped on the other side of the fire, out of breath. His joy left him and horror seized him. He trembled. From one temple to the other, from one horizon to the other, within his ribs, in this dead city, in his martyred flesh, the fly was still buzzing and defying him. He no longer knew if he was crazy or if he was hearing things. His head went beyond the roundness of the sky, exploding into the infinite. Annette's face appeared to him, her wandering braids shining brightly like two black suns. The wind pushed the fire toward him. A whirlwind of smoke crossed him. He couldn't take any more. With his two thumbs he pushed the two buttons, one after the other.

He collapsed in the laboratory. Essaillon loosened his gauges, wiping his hands in his beard, and called the women.

For a scientist, the spirit of observation is never completely extinguished, whatever may be the circumstances. In spite

of his sufferings and in spite of his delirium, St. Menoux had
seen, almost unconsciously, the smoke crossing him at the
moment when he stopped the vibrator. He had time to murmur: "Carbon oxide" before he fainted.

Essaillon bled him white, transfusing his blood with Annette's. Peter urinated black for three days. The contact of
his skin soiled the sheets. When his covers were removed, an
odor of smoked bacon rose to the nostrils. The infinite
resources of the invalid's science were right about the poisoning, but he still could not cure Peter's head cold.

Spring was peeking through the trees when Peter got up
again. His skin remained veined with long gray tracks.

The flowered garden hastened his convalescence. In the
evening, while undressing, he sometimes looked dreamily at
the fold of his elbow where Annette's blood had penetrated
him and caressed the flesh, which showed no trace of the
miracle, with his bony fingers. Little by little, during these
slow days of recovery, he felt invaded again by the image of
the young girl. His benumbed mind let his feelings expand.
Stretched out on a chaise longue, his hands hanging in the
grass, he saw, between his half-closed lids, Annette, descending the porch steps. She was carrying in her hands a
steaming bowl of a mild remedy. He closed his eyes, feigning
sleep, to hear her approaching steps on the gravel and to feel
her face bent over his. He waited for her to call his name,
sweetly and then for her caress. First letting her repeat it,
he opened his eyes whose irises took on the color of a flaxen
flower, growing in diameter each day. He already no longer
dared to look at her. She sat down next to him, legs crossed,
among the yellow and white flowers in the grass. She carefully watched him until he drank to the bottom of the bowl.
If he extended a hand toward her, she neither frightened nor
encouraged him. She did not know how to help timid boys.
She was as simple as a flower.

As the days passed, he felt closer to her. The month of May
approached its end and spring gave him back his strength.

One evening when he could not sleep, he swore to himself that tomorrow he would tell the young girl—tell her what? He turned over in his bed. How difficult it was! Wouldn't tender words sound grotesque coming from his mouth? "I love you, I love you, do you love me?"

"My friend Peter," said Essaillon at breakfast, "you are cured. I have prepared your new trip. I believe that you can leave as soon as you have finished your coffee."

He dusted his beard. They secluded themselves in the laboratory. St. Menoux had a confused memory of his last expedition. Whatever the dangers were, they were unable now to stop what they had begun. He was impassioned by the great venture. The obese scientist's words had inspired him to action. His sentimental thoughts subsided. He almost felt relieved to have to put them aside. He slipped on the diving suit. He was going to search further than the year 3000 for the survivors of the great cataclysm.

The next day he advanced one century more. Then two, three and five. What he saw and reported to the invalid appeared so bewildering to him that they agreed together to make a gigantic leap ahead in order to immediately discover the destiny of their distant grandchildren.

If electricity had disappeared and the civilization of the machine had ended, a new force had been born. Humanity, which had learned how to use it, had survived such an evolution that the two men did not dare to foresee the end result.

St. Menoux knew that when he pushed the departure button this time, he would be leaving for a voyage of a hundred thousand years. On the eve of his departure, he had a crewcut because his hair, which had turned dark with the smoke, was growing back light at the roots, giving him the appearance of a woman who dyes her hair and then neglects herself.

Part II

THE ENTOMOLOGICAL VOYAGE

1

Report of Peter St. Menoux to Noel Essaillon
on his voyage in the year 100,000

When I decided to write down what I saw, I realized the difficulties of my task. The use of adjectives is unfamiliar to me. The language of mathematics, to which I am accustomed, requires relatively few words, which are addressed to the intelligence and do not excite our emotions at all. I fear, in my awkwardness at using a descriptive style, of using too dry a description and painting a poor picture. The extraordinary world which was opened to me to explore defies our vocabulary. I will try to be exact.

I left the laboratory on June 6, 1942, at 10:27 A.M. with my apparatus adjusted to arrive at the same hour of the same day in the same season.

I was not unaware that these divisions of our time might not perhaps correspond to those of the thousandth century. The movement of the stars is not unchangeable. Days and seasons could have changed in length. Was I going to find the sun and the moon again? Was I going to find Earth again? I expected the worst.

I arrived lying down. Two dark caves wandered above my glasses. The nostrils of some monster was occupied in scenting me. Terrified, I was going to press on the vibrator when I recognized the muzzle of a cow. I do not particularly like these absurd beasts, but the presence of this one overwhelmed me with joy. How could I dream of a more pacific being to welcome me?

Between her ears I noticed an extraordinary blue sky, so pure and so clear that it seemed painted on a canvas. I noticed that the cow resembled my housekeeper. I was very occupied in listening, in smelling and in looking.

I fell into an atmosphere of a great peacefulness. An odor of cut grass filtered through my head cold. I heard a strange concert, a melange of a few sharp whistles which crossed each other on the powerful foundation of the peal of organ basses. This last sound seemed to come from the depths of the earth. The ground below me was vibrating from it.

Such were my first impressions in the new world, those that overcame me in a second, before I had the time to move: the muzzle of a cow, a piece of blue sky, the calmness of the air, a green odor, a bunch of whistles and the ground which trembled as at the passing of a subway.

I gave a tap on the cow's muzzle. She wandered off, abandoning me. I saw the brave beast in her entirety and was stupefied. Only one udder hung between the four rigid legs, ending with a single teat level with the ground. This udder, pink and round, looked like the huge breast of a woman. I estimated its capacity at about four gallons. I was moved. From the bottom of my being some memories, unconscious until then, arose. I relived the fleshy wet nurse to whom my sick mother had entrusted me and I recalled the warmth of the enormous globe from which I was nourished. Impatient with my sentimentality, I got up, consumed with curiosity. I immediately saw proof of man's presence.

Around me about fifty similar cows grazed in the thick grass. The plain continued into the horizon. In this green stretch of land were rows of gray cones, all the same, it seemed, rising about three to four yards high and lined up in two perpendicular directions like millstones in a field extending to infinity. The regularity of their spacing, form and dimensions confirmed that these constructions were the work of human hands.

A furtive noise made me turn around. Confused, I found myself opposite a man. He was naked.

I prepared to disappear, but he passed by, he even bumped me slightly, letting on that he noticed my existence. His glance slipped over me with an inorganic indifference. I had the frightening impression of being looked at by a ghost, a corpse, or a god.

Several men followed the first one, similar to him in their nudity and their calm. They walked with large, slow, heavy steps, letting their long arms hang like tools at rest. They arrived one behind another, not speaking and looking at nothing. Their skin was rough, the color of old wood, without a whisker nor a hair.

If you suddenly found yourself opposite one of your fellow-creatures deprived of clothes, where would you immediately look? I did not escape this reflex, due no doubt to obscure repressed instincts. But I could see nothing. The bottom of these brown bellies was smooth and naked. I told myself that, after all, in a thousand centuries the reproductive organ could have changed its place. Yet I searched in vain and this search brought many other surprises. The buttock muscles of these beings were joined in a single semispherical mass, polished like old leather. The anus also had apparently disappeared.

On the contrary, the chest developed toward the lower part at the expense of a reabsorbed abdomen. The ribs descended to the thighs. The man of year 100,000 had no more intestines!

The slow file of asexual beings dispersed into the field. Each one placed himself in front of a cow and began to whistle on a single note, shrilly and continuously, like a whistling tea-kettle in the early morning. The cow interrupted her meal, raised her head, and followed the melancholy whistler.

In a body, the shepherds and their beasts moved in the direction of the nearest cone. I followed them. The thick leaves of grass were crushed under my feet and spit out a frothy juice. Fringes of green foam hung from the snouts of the cows. In the distance I saw other groups of men and beasts which were directed toward the cones or stood away from them.

I walked beside the shepherds and around them, looking at them as frcely as I liked. They continued to ignore me. They measured about six feet tall, a little more or a little less, varying from one individual to the next. Their squat necks bore little heads whose naked skulls shone as much as their behinds. Their eyes were fixed like those of hens and their noses reduced in volume but very open. Their mouths were only toothless holes in the blocks of the jaws, which were soldered one to the other. Only their lips preserved their mobility.

Considering the long chest, which swelled from the shoulders to the hipbone, the mouth incapable of chewing and the absence of the anus, I wondered about the problem of their nutrition. I also thought at the same time that it was easier for them than for us, their unfortunate ancestors, to reach Paradise. No sex, no stomach, no lust, no gluttony! There remained very few occasions for them to sin.

Without losing time, we continued our way toward the cone. I was already accustomed to my new companions. I felt a sympathy for them which was perhaps a corruption of some paternal instinct. The air was very mild; the sun shone in the clear sky. Troops of pink animals, which I thought I recognized as pigs, romped here and there in the plain. Some groves added more somber spots on the solid green of the countryside. My look rested on the depth and the mellowness of the color of the grass. My eyes soaked it in and were cleansed of the fatigue of hours of work under the lamp and the bitterness of sleepless nights. The whistles of the cowherds pierced the air. The ground continued to hum. With each step, long vibrations rose up to my thighs.

Was it the warmth of the air, the odor of the crushed grass, or the infatuation of the monotonous concert? I felt my mind becoming sluggish little by little. My astonishment before the new world faded softly, my curiosity diminished and disappeared. Curiosity at what? Had I not always known

this decor, these beings, my brothers? Was I not similar to
them, a man like them? A humble, passive, happy member
of a great human family? My breathing became slower and
calmer and my heart beat at a slower rhythm. Without thinking about it, I arranged myself at the end of the line. I let my
arms hang down. I began to walk in long slow steps and began to whistle.

My shrill, short whistle jarred so disagreeably the others
that I stopped short, as one awakens after having let oneself
give in to a need in a wet dream.

Frightened out of this torpor which had seized me, I shook
myself and promised to guard myself. My peaceful companions continued on their way. They seemed not to have
heard me at all. I approached the last one and shouted in his
ear, "How are you?" Maybe I could have found a more
original question, but it was the first phrase that came to my
lips. Besides, I was not waiting for an answer, but a reflex.
Nothing happened. The shepherd did not budge. I put my
hand on his shoulder. He didn't feel it any more than a statue
feels the pigeon who perches in its bronze hair. I was prepared, all prudence lost, to strike him with my fist when,
brusquely, all of the men who made up the company turned
toward me with one movement and saw me for the first time.
Terror widened their round eyes and astonishment widened
their mouths. No less frightened, I placed my finger on the
button of the vibrator. The gesture of my arm caused a
panic. The shepherds fled as fast as their legs could carry
them, uttering shrill female cries. The abandoned cows remained in place. One of them moved gently.

The panic had reached instantaneously the entire square
plain enclosed by the four cones between which I found myself. The cowherds left their flocks, fleeing straight ahead and
shouting like beaten dogs. They ran in every direction, stopped
short, left in another direction, and ran into each other. They
finished by reaching, after one hundred zigzags, the border of
the alerted square. Those who cleared its invisible border,
immediately regained their calm, like fish thrown back into

water. Around this square, normal life continued. No one among the beings who continued their slow occupations there seemed to notice the trouble which reigned beside them.

The humming which rose from the earth stopped suddenly. The outcries of the shepherds redoubled and their flight accelerated. I myself felt invaded by an unknown terror, of which I did not know the cause. I guessed that a frightful danger was going to appear. Without waiting any longer, I pushed the button on the vibrator.

One second later, the earth began to tremble at the sound of ten thousand drums beating the signal to charge somewhere within its depths. This noise approached gradually, moving from the place beneath my feet and concentrated toward the four cones situated at the corners of the panicked square of plain.

At the base of each cone, there opened a hole similar to a tunnel entrance. I saw files of individuals whose looks made me shudder coming out of these doors. At a height double mine, and as large as elephant's buttocks, they advanced with heavy steps in rows of four. They accentuated their walk by striking their colossal chests with their enormous fists. Each blow reverberated like the shock of a mallet on an empty barrel. The blows were what made the noise that had so terrified me.

I blessed the vibrator which allowed me to escape these monsters. I had no doubt that they had come out of the earth to destroy me. They too were naked, their bodies an assemblage of gigantic bones and unlimited muscles. Like the timid shepherds, they seemed to have neither intestines nor sex. Their ribs descended down to their thighs, similar to arches of a bridge.

They were still coming from the wide-open doors. Walking with the sluggishness of pachyderms, they formed a living wall between the four cones. In a magnificent united movement they turned toward the center of the square that they had just formed. They then stopped beating their chests, unfolded their arms, and began to advance while uttering cries that sounded like a combination of the trumpeting of elephants and the cries of turkeys, multiplied a thousand times. To their arms, which hung to the ground, were attached deformed hands. The index finger and the middle finger, the third finger and the little finger were joined so as to form only two fingers, as thick as an athlete's arm, to which was opposed a thumb just as large. They ended in sharp claws.

On top of these bodies, the heads with the polished skulls seemed tiny. Facial characteristics were almost entirely erased. Their inset eyes, without lashes or brows, looked straight ahead. Two holes replaced the nose, the outer ears had disappeared, and the chin rested on a muscular neck placed like a pyramid on the shoulders ready to carry the load of Atlas.

I placed my hands on the earphones to still the noise which shattered my eardrums. But the howlings passed through my phantom flesh, filling my brain. I had to appeal to reason to calm my nervous system.

While the warriors advanced to meet each other toward the center of the square, others continued to come out from the cones, forming new files and marching on the tracks of the first ones.

Several herds of cows were in the way of the deployed army. Since their shepherds had abandoned them, the good milkers had not moved. They turned their heads this way and that, looking at the void with their large sad eyes, and mooing in the same melancholy voice as cows of our time.

The roaring warriors advanced, their arms held out, their claws settling in the tender flesh of the cows. Milk mingled with blood flowed in pink streams. The quadrupeds were torn to pieces instantly. The first rank of killers did not even stop. The following line seized some pieces and made fragments of them. The third wave transformed the fragments to pulp. The pigs faced the same destiny, as well as about twenty shepherds who had not had time to escape. When the first opposing ranks met on the slaughter field, they began to tear each other apart with the same vigor and the same cries.

Soon all that remained was the third reserve, occupied in tearing the fragments of the corpses into shreds.

I trembled in horror. Nothing could escape such a death mechanism. Nothing except the imponderable being which I had become thanks to the vibrator. What would have remained of me if I had not made use of this providential instrument?

The surviving warriors had ceased howling. They now growled like satiated beasts and reassembled in the center of the terrain. I turned my back to them and fled with a single leap up to the closest cone's door. Near this opening stood a warrior smaller than the others. He looked at the operations from afar, his half-closed hands placed in front of his eyes like field glasses. On his forearms, four tufts of white hair had grown in the form of stars.

I turned again toward the countryside covered with debris and sticky with blood. The reason for the slaughter—myself —remained. They had forgotten it. A great number of innocent beings had perished. Even the grass was destroyed. I admired how purely the traditions of war had preserved themselves over one thousand centuries.

The opening in the cone was almost the size of a cathedral portal. Yet I saw no way to close it. I had to cross nearly twenty yards to clear the thickness of the earth wall. Before me opened three alleys. The one to the left rose, another to the right descended and the third one, in the middle, disappeared into the burrow.

The warriors who re-entered from the battle, covered with blood, plunged in rows of four into the alley on the right. The man with the stars now walked at their head and swelled his torso. Some shepherds arrived, whistling their cows. They went into the central alley. I followed them.

A soft glimmer replaced the daylight. It came from a multitude of phosphorescent mushrooms which were growing on the walls with a strange speed. I saw them growing in a few seconds from the size of a pea to that of an apple and then wither. From their carcasses would spring new shoots.

They were squeezed, overlapped in a continuous palpitation of cold flame, hanging from the ceiling in heavy clusters immediately reabsorbed and ceaselessly growing.

The avenue emerged into a vast, circular vaulted room, illumined by the same light. On the ground, some bluish goatskin bottles, some of which seemed full and others empty, were arranged in rows on a layer of dry grass. I estimated their number to be about two or three thousand.

One of the shepherds who entered with me, leading his cow toward one of these limp bottles, put the animal's teat into a hole of the receptacle. With astonishment I heard a sucking noise. I approached. It was not a hole, but a mouth which sucked at the beast's udder. Around this mouth was a kind of human face, flat as a pancake, a lunar face without a skull nor a neck, scarcely distinct from the abdomen in which the breast emptied itself.

The mouth sucked like a starved baby. The soulless eyes expressed a kind of passive pleasure tinted with brutishness. They reminded me of the expression that one sees on men seated alone at restaurant tables, who neither read nor speak and are only occupied in chewing.

I heard the gurgling of the liquid which flowed into the interior of the starved being. On all sides of its stomach hung limp arms and legs, withered to the scale of a doll.

Sick to my stomach, I had to recognize the truth: these pouches scattered on the straw, these receptacles, these brainless stomachs without muscles and without bones, they too were men. This monster I was walking on with my invisible boots was perhaps born from my blood.

The meal ended. The cow empty and the man-stomach full, the shepherd withdrew the teat from the mouth with the noise of a popped cork. A bubble rose from the circular lips and burst. Translucid eyelids slowly closed the flat eyes. A lapping made the abdomen's skin quiver. The being was digesting.

Everywhere in the huge room the same operation was being carried out. Each empty stomach was filled. One thousand

mouths kissed the teats. The stomachs gurgled, the shepherds
whistled softly to their musing cows and the organ's rumbling
sound rose again from the earth. I calmed myself, regained
the tranquillity of mind indispensable for observation.

The first thing I noticed was the lack of manure. These
individuals made up of intestines possessed no anuses, just
like the cowherders and the soldiers. I concluded that the
digestion for them was a total assimilation, without waste
products.

In the center of the room stood a circular platform, a kind
of bandstand on which I saw something move as I approached.

Three creatures of the same size, very thin, almost thread-
shaped, were holding hands and moving in a slow circle with
their faces turned toward the outside.

These were still men who turned in front of me taking
large steps with their spindly legs. To reassure myself about
this, I looked at their feet, so similar to human feet of our
time, and their hands, which knotted in the eternal gesture
of friendship. But what strange heads terminated their bodies!
One of these three creatures moved his ears, which were as
large and as long as banana-tree leaves. He pointed these immense pink organs toward all the corners of the room, as if
he wanted to capture the slightest murmur. The second creature possessed a nose like an ivory horn, split into two vast
nostrils, whose wings palpitated without stopping like those of
a bat. From the skull of the third one emerged three tentacles,
three little serpents, which unfolded and twisted in the air,
each one ending with a whitish protuberance. I was guessing
at the nature of these appendages when one of them brushed
me and I saw an eye at its extremity, like a button at the end
of a thread. This being projected three eyes into space, swinging them back and forth, aiming them toward the ceiling,
projecting them over its shoulders and lowering them level
to the ground in a continuous search of some vision.

The three beings uttered, with a half sigh, a monotonous
melancholic lament. They turned around with large slow

steps, hand in hand, wailing in a voice which resembled a
child crying far into the night. The ears of one, the eyes of
the other, the nose of the third, the feet of all three and their
swinging arms moved to the slow rhythm of their murmur.

In spite of their deformed faces they kept a human and
desolate appearance. They seemed conscious of their hideous-
ness, both resigned to their destiny and inconsolable. But I
think I am giving too beautiful a description out of my own
compassion. One sees ugly people every day who seem unfortunate and whom one pities, but who would not change
their noses for the one of Adonis.

I turned away from the trio, suspecting that I had guessed
their role. Furnished with organs of extremely developed
senses, they were in charge of searching out all abnormality
in their field of vision, hearing and smell.

I had met muscular beings, shepherds and soldiers, who
were charged with a precise task and whose senses only per-
ceived what was related to their work.

I had next seen some stomachs who took enough food
each for four hundred people. No doubt they were eating for
the gutless men.

Finally, I examined some creatures who looked, listened
and smelled for the entire community. I began to understand
the operation of the city. However, before expressing an
hypothesis, it was necessary for me to push my investiga-
tions further.

Since I had penetrated the cone, I heard—above the gur-
glings and the hiccups of the stomachs, and the desolate
murmur of the central trio—a distant concert of frightful
cries. I left the large room across the ceiling and reached a
second room scarcely smaller. It seemed as though I had
entered into hell. A red light flickered around me like the
flames of a funeral pyre. Red mushrooms swarmed over the
walls and lit up with a fire of sunset some beings who were
struggling on the ground. I had to accustom myself for a few
seconds to the changing light. On the stable-litter of dry grass

there were aligned some stomach-men of a new variety, furnished with solid arms, hooked hands and a shark's mouth.

A shepherd followed by a pig approached one of these man-jaws. The latter extended his arms in the blood-colored air, hooked on to the howling animal, carried it to his mouth and suddenly cut its two shanks. In less than one minute, he had entirely devoured it.

I must confess that I had not succeeded, in the course of my previous voyages, in suppressing my expression of amazement, or horror or joy. What I had already seen did not prevent me from being moved by what I was seeing now. I strove, however, to always keep a clear mind.

I therefore pitied these pink pigs and I leaned over one of them in sympathy. It was very much our familiar pig, the innocent companion of St. Anthony. An animal perhaps more perfect than us, since in these one thousand centuries he had not changed at all, while man had been transformed so radically. He had, however, lost his tail—judged useless no doubt.

I suppressed my ill-considered pity—do we not also love the sausage?—and left without lingering any longer in this bloody place.

On the floor above, lit in soft green, I found a third variety of stomach-men, nourished with fruits. Farmers passed among them, each one carrying two apples or two pears, one in each hand. I was astonished at this waste of time and work. I couldn't recall having seen until then either a tool nor a container in the hands of the men of the thousandth century. I concluded that they possessed no industry and that the class of craftsmen had disappeared.

The fourth room was lit with gold-colored mushrooms. This joyous light cheered me. In the center of the room a large earth tub had been built. Some paths climbed its sloping sides. Some agriculturists climbed them with a light step, almost dancing. Arriving at the summit, they threw into it one single bunch of grapes, after having pulverized it between their hands, and then turned around to get another. The contents of the vat were fermenting. The overflow ran into several hundreds of little trenches of earth down to the funnel-shaped mouths of the new stomach-men. These men had red noses and little gay eyes. They belched. They resembled the common man of the twentieth century more than all the others.

In each one of the rooms, an alert trio revolved in its identical melancholy circle at the same rhythm with the same lament. I found another of them at the top of the cone on the tiny exterior platform to which the rising alley led. It surveyed the countryside. It was certainly he who had discovered me. My green diving suit which mingled with the grass had allowed me to escape the looks of the Argus. But as soon as I began to whistle and shout, the banana-tree ears had heard me. By what mysterious means had the shepherds immediately known my presence and had the warriors received the order to destroy me? My first visit to the year 100,000 did not tell me. Since my explorations into previous centuries, however, I have discovered the force which allows the new men to communicate among themselves. I still do not know the way in which they use it.

I looked off into the distance from this high place. Cones similar to the one that I had just visited rose at regular distances in an infinite number. Their points transformed the horizons into blades of saws. Each one of them was crowned with the same grotesque and desolate trinity.

The group of farmers slowly moved close to the cows and pigs and groves of fruit trees. I no longer saw any trace of the massacre. The miraculous grass had already grown back. The prosperity of the pastures erased the memories of death. Other cows grazed in the fields. The crowd of farmers slowly moved among the white and pink animals, soft pink spots on a sea of deep green. The concert of whistles and subterranean organ filled the air with tranquilizing vibrations. The sun shone in an enamel sky. The new world gave the appearance of serene peace.

I resolved to take some pictures. I stopped the vibrator and took out my camera. I re-encountered the shock of the powerful odor of the grass which I had almost forgotten. It penetrated my head and my flesh, with the rhythm of long hummings which rose from the earth and invaded me to the bottom of my boots. I felt myself becoming green. The warmth of the air bathed me like water, overwhelming me with well-being. The same torpor which had already invaded me slowed my movements and dulled my curiosity. The camera drooped at the end of my arm. I reacted quickly and continued my filming.

Behind me the watchful trio had accelerated its circle. To a precipitating cadence, its wailing rose to a shriek. The horn-nose smelled me noisily at each turn. The ears encircled my head. The tentacle-eyes enveloped me in arabesques; their distressed eyeballs passing like lightening in front of my face.

I heard the drum-chest resounding in the earth's entrails. I imagined the walk of the ruthless warriors along the spiral trail. I did not wait for their arrival.

Annette was alone in the laboratory when St. Menoux returned. Her father was dozing in the parlor near the open window, his nose resting in his beard. Annette arranged the instruments he used, the bottles of thick liquids. She closed a closet, humming while crossing the room. She had loosened her hair, which rolled down onto her shoulders in heavy living curls.

The image of the tall man filled her so completely that she was scarcely conscious of thinking of him. At first she worried about his departure, but she quickly reassured herself, certain of seeing him again as one is certain of seeing the sun rise.

He appeared before her vertically. She uttered a little cry and put her two hands on her heart.

"Oh," she said, "you frightened me."

He did not answer, nor move. He looked at her.

In his mind, images of the men of the thousandth century were stirring. The hideous stomachs, the shark mouths, the sauntering eyes, the hook hands, the monstrous chests, and the soldered rears danced a nightmare in his memory. Now he was welcomed on his return by the most marvelous creature of his time: a young woman.

As he looked at her, he discovered the harmonious miracle of her forms, her complexion and her movements. How large her eyes are! he thought. How pink and soft her lips are! How pale her cheeks are against her black hair!

He marveled at belonging to a world which possessed millions of such creatures. All around the earth, in day and night, at dawn and at twilight, blossom young girls. This one, simple, tender, perfumed by her beauty and youth, this one was promised to him. Now he knew it.

"Annette," he said in a rather hollow voice, "I will never be able to thank God enough for having made you so beautiful."

He approached her. Annette's eyes grew larger, exceeding her face and filling the sky.

Peter threw off his gloves and placed his hands on her round shoulders, which felt like the heat of a dove. He closed his arms around the girl, pulling her close to his heart which grew light and immense.

His clenched arms softly relaxed. Annette eased her head close against the boy's chest. Her cheeks were flushed. She leaned back and saw far above her a face of green wool and two blue eyes behind windows.

She heaved a great sigh to empty a little of the happiness that was choking her.

He saw below him an overwhelmed face held out toward him—a parenthesis of shadow between two hidden breasts. In Annette's eyes he saw tears well up, spreading, shining and slowly closing her eyelids.

He believed that night had come. He called out to her. "Annette!"

She opened her illuminated eyes and smiled with infinite tenderness and he was reassured forever.

Continuation of St. Menoux's Report

In two months of our time, I crossed one thousand centuries thirty times and came back thirty times from this future. The vibrator permitted me to mingle in the lives of our descendants without any danger. I accumulated observations. Now I will try to synthesize them.

In the course of some of the voyages which preceded my first exploration into the year 100,000, I could follow the beginning of the evolution undergone by humanity from the year 2052. In that year, energy, which we call electricity, disappeared.[1]

It was a catastrophe. Nine out of ten men died. Death came more quickly and more effectively than during the most perfected wars.

The survivors, I soon learned, used a new force, born in their brains. Perhaps electricity had only transformed itself. Certain indications lead me to believe, however, that the new energy already exists in our time. Yet we are unaware of its existence and have not tried to discover it: the power of our machines satisfies us.

All of the human beings after 2052 were more or less gifted with this force. However few among them knew how to make the best use of it. The first to use it rationally was a farmer named Lucky who found field work laborious. He suc-

---

[1]Here St. Menoux, in spite of his scientific mind, commits an error. In *Ravage*, which is the account of this event, of its consequences for humanity and of the world which is collapsing. The author, who studied the facts as much as was possible, arrived at this conclusion: electricity did not disappear, it simply ceased in an instant across the entire world to manifest itself in its usual forms. Thus bodies, which up to then were conductors, suddenly were no longer. There was no more current, no more lightning, no more sparks, no more electric batteries nor storage cells. All motors, including atomic motors and solar motors with photoelectric cells, stop at the same instant in the entire world. Suddenly all vehicles stopped, all airplanes fell, all factories ceased to operate. No more transportation, no more current, no more water, no more living in the immense cities which held all of the population of the twenty-first century. It was a frightful collapse and happened because of this simple phenomena: one of the natural forces to which man was accustomed suddenly changed. What were the causes of this change? The author could not tell you. But would you know how to tell him what makes electricity what it is today?

ceeded in making himself obeyed at the first word and then
without speaking, not only by men but by animals and finally
by objects. The tools which he needed leapt into his hand.
Soon he no longer called for the tools, but only his pipe or
jug. He remained on his bench in the sun. Twenty men
worked for him. He enslaved an entire village and grew fat.

This happened around the year 3110. King Honoré the
Third, forty-fifth successor of the patriarch François, made
Lucky appear before him and condemned him to be burned
alive. Lucky arose laughing from the ashes of the pyre. The
people who had spit on him berated Honoré and installed
Lucky, the miracle worker, on the throne.

The new sovereign was a bon vivant. He wanted his subjects to bring him happiness. All his subjects, without excep-
tion. He began by seeking out a few powerful brains, con-
stituting by their union a kind of storage battery of mental
energy. This organism carried the name of "Brain-trust" in
the language of the age. The men with weak brains, that is to
say the multitude, submitted to his will. He even ordered the
king himself and absorbed him. He became the master of
humanity.

From this moment, the men who composed it lost their
individuality. They could not profit from their power. Their
common will, directed toward the good fortune of their contemporaries, and which inexorably guided these people to a
strange obligatory bliss, forced them to yield their individuality under the law. In spite of themselves, they became the
servants of the city they created. Their number increased;
their collective power increased prodigiously. Their personal
power was nonexistent. The force emanating from them
seemed to have its own life. The principles of justice and
social welfare, imagined in an exacting way by men's brains,
were liberated from the human authority which had never
known how to apply them. They formed themselves into in-
dependent energy. They reigned, however, with perfect
strength.

For the good of all, the new force alloted to each man a

precise task, modified his body in order to make his work easier for him and diminished the power of his senses with the goal of avoiding for him not only all sorrow, but all sensation useless to the operation of the city.

Thus, in the course of the centuries, man evolved into the cell of a perfect social body. He only saw, heard, or smelled that which concerned his task, from which nothing diverted him. He knew neither suffering nor regret nor desire.

The globe's population multiplied. It modified its habitat according to the same principle of justice. Attacked by a formidable manpower, the mountains were demolished, oceans filled, rivers buried and the earth leveled. An internal circulation superceded the exterior cycle of water: rain-river-sea-cloud-rain. The streams and rivers flowed in the interior of the globe in a perpetual movement maintained by the temperature differences of the underground. Canals dug by men irrigated the meadows and orchards above, giving to the air, through the medium of the plants, the humidity necessary to life. It transported the heat of the central core toward the poles and the hemispheres threatened by winter. Thus was abolished this natural inequality which made a Southern European benefit from a temperate climate while his Eskimo brother, born equal in rights, suffered the rigors of the cold.

Our earth was no longer recognizable. Completely flat, completely lukewarm, it offered no attraction to the tourist. Yet there are no more tourists in the thousandth century, no more idlers, no more men who egotistically profit from others' work and pass their time at will. Each one works for all and all work for each, on or below a land deprived of the picturesque. No more storms, no more waterfalls, no more lofty mountains, no more gentle hills. The plain everywhere. The sun always.

Wherever I crossed the earth, I saw it staked out in rows of cones where the stomach-men lived. Between these innumerable similar constructions, the ground was covered with pastures and forests of fruit trees. The new man does not practice farming, properly speaking. He is content to exterminate all the useless or detrimental vegetables. He destroyed equally the birds, fish, reptiles, bacteria, insects, and arachnoids, worms and mollusks, protozoans and hydras, sponges and echinoderms, arthropodes and ascidians; all the inhabitants of the waters, of the air and of the earth for which he had no use. Mammals had been reduced to two species—cows and pigs, which became herbivorous.

Under the green crust of ground, garnished with cones, millions of galleries pierce the globe in all directions. Water vapor and fire circulate in them, watched by the underground workers.

These prodigious works, which our machines could never make and of which no brain of our time could conceive, were thought out and directed by the collective energy and executed by the multitude, without the help of any tool. Oceans were filled with handfuls of earth and mountains were scraped by hand. But what hands! The frontal limbs of the workers who watch over the maintenance and the new growth of the underground canals had become burrowing spades, made of a horn harder than steel.

One should not forget, on the other hand, that the new humanity used an enormous number of workers and that their works were executed little by little with a patience and persistence that our world, which is constantly occupied in changing regimes and ideals, could never imagine.

A few voyages into the time which separates us from the year 100,000 revealed the approximate duration of certain of these projects. It took eleven thousand years for human erosion to demolish the Alps. The last leaf of crab grass had been pulled out in the year 98,000 and the fly was crushed after fifteen centuries of merciless war. A perfect world could not be constructed from one day to the next.

The workers of the underground are deprived of respiratory apparatus as well as a digestive tract and reproductive organs. Their body is only a great mass of muscle. Their flattened heads help them to pile stones and rocks. Those who work near the central fire move in boiling water among the flames, splashing in the lava without feeling the slightest pain. The collective energy which reigns over the city sheathes them with a kind of insulating armour. Certain peoples of our time seem to have known this immunity. Travelers have seen Hindu fakirs or African witchdoctors walking barefoot on flaming coals without getting burned. This is what inclines me to suppose that this mental energy could have been cultivated in our time if electricity had not satisfied us.

The society of the year 100,000 is therefore governed by an inexorable justice. Individualism, for which we are so criticized, is no longer even conceivable there. Man has forgotten himself as an individual. He no longer possesses sensation nor personal thought. He lives for and by his brother.

However, even in this very organized world, there reigns a flagrant inequality: some work without eating, others eat without working. That would establish a certain relationship between this century and ours, if the food ingested by the stomach-men did not profit all. That is not the case for us.

The warrior class seems to have the best of it because there is not much left for him to exterminate. The valiant soldiers spend their time sleeping standing, always in rows of four, in immense underground rooms. Along with the cultivators, they are in charge of the respiratory function of the social body. Their rumblings make this organ noise which makes the ground vibrate.

The warriors and cultivators breathe, the stomach-men digest and the alert trios feel, see and listen for all. I still could not discover how the profit of the digestive system, respiratory system or sensation-gathering system by one of these overdeveloped organs is transmitted from one to the other. No doubt, all is deposited into the common reserve of energy from which the new humanity suckles. But how does each one draw from it? The men of the thousandth century do not seem to possess any new organ evolved for this function. I suppose that their nervous systems, or what remains of their brains, are directly irrigated by this flow—a new kind of collective blood.

If I wasn't careful, I would very quickly have submitted to the hold of this new force. When the vibrator was stopped, I had to pay attention not to let my personality lose consciousness. I surprised myself by whistling with the cows, snoring with the soldiers and holding out greedy hands toward the little chubby pigs. The slightest interruption awoke me, though, and I came to my senses.

I did not find a trace anywhere of a controlling organ. Was the brain trust, surpassed by its will, reabsorbed little by little? I hope to get an answer to this question in the course of my next voyages. Another question, no less important, is raised: how do the new men reproduce? I have not met any women in these advanced years. If I use the word "man" to describe the beings I saw, it is for want of a more appropriate terms. They are all deprived of sex, completely atrophied.

I have not forgotten that my explorations have no other goal than to discover the secret of happiness, if not for man, at least for men. Have they finally found it? It is true that they are not unhappy. That is already an achievement. Yet, are they happy? I cannot answer this question before discovering if they know love.

2

Each time he returned from the future, St. Menoux was happily reunited with Annette. She represented for him all that in our archaic humanity, fraught with such frightful hazards and spotted with so many miseries, still gives to life a taste of marvelous sweetness.

Her long hair, falling over her shoulders in aimless curls, her gracious virgin breasts and her calves with tender curves all completed a lovely whole. Her black eyes, so large and so radiant, seemed to St. Menoux less for seeing than for being contemplated. She was dressed simply but beautifully and delicately perfumed. Her little feet in finely made shoes, her two hands crossed and the movement of a tight dress around her waist and hips seemed wonderful to the young man when he came back from the new world.

He loved her for what she was and for all that he no longer found in the future city. She epitomized the spring flowers that push their gentle faces toward the sun, birds that ruffle their feathers in the sunrise, drops of water thrown from streams on blades of grass, the rose cheeks of the mountains in twilight and the design of starfish on the sand.

He loved her more each day and told her so when he was alone with her. He spoke little but never tired of touching her. He asked his fingers to confirm for him the wonder of his eyes. He placed his hand on the roundness of her hip or shoulder and plunged his open fingers into the freshness of her hair. He drew her against him to feel her with all his body, leaned over and placed his lips on her white forehead.

Then he felt penetrated by the warmth of the world. He forgot his large bones and his too-short sleeves. He became part of a universal joy, like a flowered branch in the May wind.

Before Essaillon, the young couple kept their distance. Peter was waiting to complete his study of the future civilization before officially asking for her hand in marriage.

Annette, for her part, knew the jealous love that her father had for her. She feared that it would hurt him to see her love someone other than himself, even if it was this faithful collaborator. She dreaded the moment when he would learn of their love. She was happy now. She delayed the moment of making him unhappy.

St. Menoux's Report (Fragments)

Did she no longer exist? Had the world become Paradise without Eve? I could not believe it. I left time after time in hope of finding her. I had covered the laboratory with photographs of women occupied with the tasks common to them: housework, cooking, and child care. I filled my eyes with them before leaving. No result. I replaced them with portraits of nursing mothers. They led me into the pastures, among my friends, the cows. I bought a series of obscene postcards from a filthy leering peddler, but I decided against using them. For men in our time, love became vice, pleasure or habit but most often distraction. In the world of the thousandth century, I had no doubt that it had returned to the simplicity of function. I finally used a scientific film. Made for medical students, it showed the vicissitudes of a difficult birth. I thus left with my mind filled with biological images and liberated from all erotic or sentimental feelings.

I arrived at the end of the day. A mountain rose some distance before me, a perfect hemisphere, obviously made by men's hands. I guessed its base diameter to be about one and a half miles. I pushed on the vibrator as soon as I arrived because a crowd was surrounding me. The beings in it were new to me. They came up to my knees. They were all rushing

in the same direction—toward the mountain. I bent down to
their level in order to see them better. They traveled through
me while running. What urgent task was calling them? For
the first time, I found myself among people who resemble us.
Was it for this reason that I found them beautiful? Their
short curly hair, their round heads, the fine features of their
faces and their well-outlined muscles reminded me of the
bronze sculpture *The Athlete* which sits on my housekeeper's
mantel between two Chinese vases. The prudish sculptor did
not provide it with virility, and the little men who surrounded
me did not possess it either. Their trampling was like the
endless herds that move along the Provence roads. The sunset rimmed their silhouette in pink, turned the dust rising
above them purple, tinted the mountain in rose. Once again I
found neither man nor woman around me. Would my new
voyage be in vain?

I threw myself ahead with a thrust of my shoulders, gliding
above the multitudes. My heartbeats raised and lowered me. I
advanced like a piece of jetsam pushed by the waves.

Soon the little beings could no longer run, no longer walk
because of their large number. They crowded together one
against another, gathered like dry figs. Their impatient feet
vainly trampled the ground. Their numberless heads undulated like a harvest in the glorious dust. I cleared this
mass and arrived at an empty space. A few yards separated the
crowd from the mountain's edge. It seemed to be stopped
there by a superior force. A violent emotion excited the
men in the first row. Behind them the new arrivals pushed
and stamped. Thousands of naked heels and shrunken toes
struck the earth. The pressed bodies slowly moved and turned
around the mound's circumference.

In the circular wall somber doors on the scale of the little
men were spaced every two yards. It was toward these doors
that they looked; it was their darkness that they searched.
From time to time one of them seemed to find the reason
for which he had come from the far horizon. He sighed a
cry of joy, left his brothers and leaped into the opening.

I leaned over to look in turn into one of these doors. What I saw astonished me. I went from one door to another, investigating about a hundred of them. Sometimes a little man traversed me like an arrow and I heard his hurried steps die in the thickness of the rampart.

Under each of these somber vaults, deep in the middle of a tunnel, palpitated a violently lit image, an image which seemed both living and untouchable, a phantom dressed in all the colors of flesh.

Here were a woman's legs, there a face, a thin flank, plump buttocks, a flat stomach, a round and soft breast, a smile, blonde hair, a dimple, a creased stomach, a beauty mark on a hip, a hand, a blue eye, a straight nose, an aquiline nose, an ankle, a shaded lip, an ear. Thousands of fragments of feminine bodies, plump or thin, ugly or beautiful, blonde or brunette, young or old. All women. All woman. The little men moved around the mound sampling, and when each met his ideal, he rushed forward, crossed the image and disappeared into the darkness. The image continued to palpitate and to offer itself to the lovers.

I decided to try filming one of these apparitions. A beautiful back with pure lines, beautiful as a fragment of an antique statue, seemed luminous enough to make an impression on the film. I stopped the vibrator, took out my camera and turned it toward the narrow door.

A violent emotion gripped me—the white shoulders had disappeared. In their place, two black eyes were looking at me, two eyes which I knew well, eyes which I love, the eyes of a woman whose name I need not mention here, but who is my whole life. They were looking at me; they were beckoning me. They shone with the most beautiful light in the world, expressing their love. My love was calling me. I heard her voice. The multitude trampled, panted, moaned. In the noise of the tide, I heard my loved one's voice, "Come, I love you, I am yours." The multitude suffered, groaned and perspired. Through its odor of a herd, I smelled the night perfume of the one who awaited me. I felt her warmth on my body. An

unbelievable energy excited me. I raised my arms to the
heavens. Blood rushed to my head. I advanced, I ran, I cried
with joy. I would take my loved one . . .

. . . I crashed brutally against the mountain wall. The
shock awoke me. My nose was bleeding inside my hood. The
door, luckily, was much too small for me. Thank God! The
spectacles were made of unbreakable glass. Before the mirage
could take hold of me again, I activated the vibrator. I had
just felt once again the power of the force which commands the new city.

I wondered what would have happened if I had been able
to clear the entrance? I decided to try to solve the mystery.
After I had passed through about one hundred feet of wall,
I emerged into an immense cupola. Some blue mushrooms lit
it like a summer sky.

A gigantic mass filled it entirely, almost to the walls. A
living mass, an enormous half-sphere which must weigh several hundreds of thousands of tons, sheltered in the mountain
like a mollusk in its shell. Its pink skin was strangely soft, as
satiny as a child's cheek or the virgin belly of a young girl.

Toward each corridor that communicated with the exterior,
the monster extended a short appendage terminating in a
soft mouth. When one of the tiny men arrived running, the
mouth opened, swallowed him and closed with a wet noise.
The appendage reabsorbed itself, the mountain of flesh swallowed its prey with a shudder of pleasure, and the mouth took
its place again before the gloomy orifice.

On going around the giant I found it the same on all sides.
It swallowed the crowd of delighted men with all of its
mouths at the rhythm of several hundred per minute. Its
thousands of lips, opening and closing, made a soft noise,
the splashing of a very smooth sea.

I decided that the impatient crowd rushing outside must
not know the abominable death awaiting it, nor the frightful trap that lay behind the mirage. Did these beings only
know the sensation of death?

While examining the giant closer, I noticed that it did not

rest on the ground but was buried in it. I had only seen the upper part. I plunged into the earth, burying myself like a stone in water.

I arrived in a huge room, lit with the same vivid light. A crowd composed of all the different males of the thousandth century was busy around me. I again heard that noise peculiar to the new times, that noise which I would like to qualify as silent—the tramp of beings who do not pronounce one word, do not utter one sigh.

On the ceiling of the room, vast as the sky, I saw, stupefied, the lower part of the mountain-being hanging, similar to the lower half of a balloon. The gaping channel at its bottom was as large as the Seine and the Champs-Elysees joined together. From this organ there emerged, slowly and endlessly, a conglomerate which crumbled as soon as it touched the ground. Each fragment began to move, flutter about, and stand up—it was a man from the new times. I saw warriors, cultivators, stomachs, underground workers, alert trios who are already holding each other by the hands and many others whom I did not recognize, rising by the thousands. They immediately divided according to type and each particular crowd went toward a different door. The cultivators carried the stomach-men folded small under their arms.

I suddenly understood the sense of all that I'd seen since my arrival. I was watching the multiplication and birth of the new men. The mountain-being crouched in its shell of earth is—I dare not say woman—is the female, it is the queen. The little people who trample impatiently in the dust are the males.

I now understood their joy. It was toward life and not death that they were rushing. How miserable my contemporaries, my brothers seemed next to them! How mean I felt. We only give ourselves to woman to recover ourselves immediately. We are full of calculations and hidden motives. After one second of abandonment, we retract into our shell of conceit and selfishness. Our distant descendants were giving themselves entirely—flesh and hide, once and for all. They did not need any male organ. The organ was their body, which dissolved totally in the breast of the woman, as a few poets and lovers of our time had wished—with the security of knowing that it was fortunately impossible—to melt into the loved object. Each one of these individuals, sacrificed by the city law, lost its existence in a climax of love to assure the continuation of the species. From this perfect union of the female and males, adult children are born who already knew what they had to do and rushed toward the place of their work.

The mirage with a thousand faces which attracted the little males toward the universal woman was perhaps the only common trait between their love and ours.

I returned to the upper room. The sacrifice continued. It must be uninterrupted, continuing day and night, like the births. I let myself slowly rise, a wisp of invisible vapor, along the rose-colored flank behind which the mystery was being accomplished. I followed its soft curve and arrived at the summit.

At the very top of the enormous mass, under the vault of the cupola, in a bed of golden hair, reposes the queen's head. Scarcely larger than one of our women's heads, she was leaning backwards with her eyes closed. Her hair, surrounding her with its waves, touched my feet with its blonde flow. The fine lines of her face, her smooth forehead, her tiny ears, and her pale complexion made her unbelievably beautiful. Her slightly hollow cheeks sheltered a moving shadow. Her closed lips outlined a smile which bathed her in mystery. She was the epitome of the beauties of all our women, and her face expressed this supreme happiness of love which approaches the anguish of death.

Like a storm, a violent expression sometimes overwhelmed the face bathed in gold, twisted her mouth and ravaged her forehead. Without opening her eyelids, she turned to the right and to the left in the pillow of her hair, struggled and then, little by little, regained her calm without my knowing whether it was the joy of the lover or the suffering of the woman in labor which has troubled her enigmatic repose.

In the course of the same voyage St. Menoux discovered several of these mountain-beings, arranged at long intervals along the line of the equator.

When he returned to Annette, he considered the destiny of the little males of the thousandth century with less enthusiasm. He looked at the girl, gracious and supple, coming and going in the house, bringing it to a harmonious order with her fairy hands, and thought happily that after having lost himself in her, he would be able to find himself before losing himself again.

Annette, for her part, tried to imagine herself as her sister in the future time. Imagining herself absorbing such a quantity of males made her suddenly feel very uneasy. She saw herself surrounded by thousands of little St. Menouxs, but her dream did not go any further. She blushed, raising her brilliant eyes toward the tall boy who resisted his desire to take her in his arms in the invalid's presence.

Essaillon was working on his *Essay On The Evolution of Mankind.* Scientific passion obscured his eyes. His collaborator's last report had overwhelmed him. He constructed a new camera, furnished with films sensitive to infrared rays. Then he closed himself in the laboratory for a few days. One beautiful morning he declared to Peter that he expected to accompany him on his next voyage.

"That's crazy!" exclaimed St. Menoux.

He threw up his arms to express his feelings and hit the electric bulb which was swinging on the end of a wire.

"Don't demolish my equipment," said Essaillon, smiling. "Why would it be crazy? I have treated an iron chair with the noelite. I will leave seated. I will arrive likewise. Once arrived, the vibrator will protect me from everything. I want to see the future world at least once."

"I understand your curiosity," said St. Menoux, shaking his head. "I still disapprove of your plan."

"Curiosity?" interrupted the scientist. "You don't quite understand, my friend. It is mainly impatience. We now know that in this strange society some work, others eat, breathe, make love, bear children or battle, but we do not yet know who thinks. Without me, I fear that you will trample around a long time before finding out."

Unconsciously he rumpled a beautiful handful of beard in each hand. His eyes became dreamy. He went on, "Now I am in a hurry to go further. It is not the year 100,000 which will give us the secret of man's happiness. I believe that this civilization is also destined to disappear. I wish to know the one which will replace it. The thousandth century is beginning to become the past for me."

In the afternoon of the same day, he entrusted Philomena with a mysterious task. She came back with a curly-headed man. The three of them closed themselves in the scientist's bedroom. When the man was gone, Essaillon called Peter and Annette.

They uttered the same exclamation of horrified surprise. The invalid's beard had been cut. A whitish chin, falling in three rows on his chest, hid his neck. In contrast to the skin of his cheeks, hidden from the light for such a long time, the skin of his pale skull seemed almost sunburned.

It was another man who revealed himself, once the hairy curtain was removed. A man more material and less glorious. For the first time, St. Menoux saw the scientist's mouth stripped of its mystery. It seemed to him both obstinate and sensual, the lower lip thick and the upper lip straight and inflexible.

"It would have bothered me in the diving suit," said the obese man pointing at the golden harvest that Philomena had gathered in a towel. "We are going to give it to the blind. There is enough there to make a good pillow."

They left. St. Menoux, standing so thin and tall, held the

enormous round scientist by the hand as he sat in his iron
chair. Annette gave the departure signal. She counted "One,
two, three!" They had practiced several times. It was a question of leaving exactly at the same time in order to arrive
likewise. On "three," they both pushed the button.

Annette, sighing, busied herself putting the laboratory in
order, preparing the next day's work and recording in a
large red notebook the results of the last experiments on the
variations of the conductibility of the noelite copper. She
hoped by her activity to chase away her worries. She thought
that it might be necessary to make a trip to 1939. Philomena
had no more white flour for pastries.

They arrived at the summit of a round mountain. From
the top of this observatory, the scientist, very moved, contemplated the new face of the earth. Liberated from weight
by the vibrator, he launched out, following St. Menoux, like
a swollen sack of warm air. They strolled around the mountain, coming upon the rush of the males toward the mirage
doors. They crossed the wall of earth with them and saw
their sacrifice. Essaillon wanted to contemplate the queen's
face. She was brunette. The light reflected in blue flames in
the twisted sea of her hair. The scientist bent before the
woman who was one thousand times taken and 100,000 times
agonized. Her pale eyelids, heavy as marble, slowly opened.
The eyes without pupils, the white statue eyes, fixed on the
two overcome men. Then they closed on their immense
dream.

The vibrators of the diving suits did not function absolutely at the same rhythm and the two men only met during
the interferences, about twenty times per second. The persistence of the retina-like images allowed them to connect these
successive images between them. They appeared like transparent but somber phantoms to each other. In order to
understand one another, they had to speak slowly. The interferences ate certain syllables while accentuating others.

They walked above the peaceful countryside. St. Menoux

had to stop twice to open his hood and blow his nose. His cold was becoming chronic and was pushing unpleasant pains up to his ears and behind his eyes.

"My poor friend, I must think seriously about finding a remedy for you!" said Essaillon.

The two companions continued their voyage, exploring underground and crossing rows of warriors who were sleeping by battalion. They saw the inexhaustible workers digging out the earth and plunging into the fire. But they met no thinking being anywhere.

They climbed again to the top of a round mountain, stopping the vibrator. Essaillon found himself seated in his faithful chair, fixed by straps on his waist.

"I brought something," he said, "which should lead us toward our goal."

He groped in his knapsack. His diving suit further aggravated the awkwardness of his short arms which he crossed painfully over his stomach. He succeeded in pulling out a large brown manila envelope.

"Let's adjust our equipment first. We are going to make a little jump ahead. Just a half hour, to give our minds the opportunity to transport us to the place we want."

He drew a photograph from the envelope and showed it to St. Menoux. It was a mountain, a kind of collage composed of images of places in the twentieth century where the mind predominates. There was the Sorbonne and Heidelberg, Oxford, the Polytechnical School in Paris, an arrangement of the Larousse Encyclopedia in twenty volumes, the last Ministry of the French Republic shown on the steps of the Elysee Palace, a kindergarten class, the facade of a prep school and the cupola of the Pedagogical Institute.

They found themselves side by side in a large vaulted room which was extremely hot. In front of them, an alert trio was revolving. Before they could be seen, the two men disappeared.

The circular room was hardly more than ten yards in diameter. In the center rose a column, around which the

sensitive trio turned. About fifty semicylindrical inches were
hollowed in the wall, from the ground up to the vault. Men
who only differed from the cultivators on the surface by the
whiteness of their skin, went from one niche to another,
seeming to survey their interiors. In each of these niches was
a pile of flattened cylindrical objects, slightly luminous.

Their pink light mingled with that of the mushrooms. These
mushrooms did not grow beyond the size of a billiard ball,
even at the peak of their development. They grew, multiplied
and died at the speed of bubbles in boiling water.

During the fraction of a second which followed their arrival, the two men smelled a sweet, sharp odor rising with the
heat. They felt as if they had just entered a stable.

The light from one of these cylindrical objects went out.
A guardsman, carefully dismantled the pile to take out the
extinguished one and left carrying it under his arm. Another
man arrived with a brilliant new object and restored the
pile to its original height.

Essaillon's phantom had already made a tour of the room
several times, floating along the walls, stopping and starting
up as if pushed by a capricious breeze.

"What do you think it is?" he squeaked, pointing to a pile
that he had just examined.

St. Menoux recalled the odor which had welcomed him and
conjectured, "Cheese?"

The scientist's shadow shook his head and said, "They're
brains!"

Peter, stupefied, had to admit it was true. He recognized,
flattened and deformed, the cerebral hemispheres, the horn
of Amon, the spur, the didymous, and the sphenoid lobes.
The isthmus of the encephalon had retracted, and the tree of
budding life, the calamus scriptorius, shuddered. The aque-
duct of Sylvius was filled with light, the cistern overflowed
with it and the pineal gland shone like an angora rabbit's eye.

The heaped brains, each enveloped in a case as transparent
as cellophane, slowly fermented and boiled with little noise.

The envelope was pierced with two rows of round holes

which crossed in the form of the letter X. Essaillon pointed
at it with a trembling finger. His voice was overcome with
emotion. "The sign of our school," he said, "the sign of the
Polytechnical School! It marks today as yesterday the pure
brains!"

St. Menoux then understood why the world of the thousandth century was so perfectly normalized. The evolution
which had transformed humanity in the course of these
100,000 years had begun in 1940. It continued inexorably
throughout all catastrophes, the brain trust continued the
work of the Committees of Organization.

The two voyagers, leaving the room, found another similar
one, then another and another. The fat man boldly went
ahead, his phantom chair stuck to his behind.

They advanced a long time without finding an end to the
cervical rooms. Passing by chance through a perpendicular
corridor, they emerged on a vast underground avenue.

On the banks of the roadside, two rows of black men
were walking with slow and heavy steps. Their skin shone
like an insect's shell. Their impassive faces seemed like ebony
masks. Each one carried a cadaver on his shoulders.

Warriors, cultivators, workers, and alert trios were going
toward some kind of tomb.

In the middle of the alley, the shining pallbearers returned,
their hands empty and their backs round. The scraping noise
of the thousands of naked feet on the beaten path reverberated against the vault, filling the avenue with a dense vibra-
tion.

Essaillon and St. Menoux mingled in the crowd of bearers.
They came with them at the edge of an immense well surrounded by a parapet. Along its walls some green mushrooms
palpitated, bursting in phosphorescent dust. A luminous and
pale cloud whirled in the abyss, from which rose a strange
and infinitely distant noise like the clamor of heinous beasts
from another world, stifled by thousands of miles of distance
and immaterial walls. It is a noise barely louder than silence,
similar to the echo of the sea in shells, but which carried a

tone of indescribable horror from the bottom of the earth
to the travelers' ears.

St. Menoux felt his hair bristle all along his skin. He wanted
to leave. Essaillon calmly looked on.

About one hundred avenues ended at the edge of the well.
The pallbearers arrived continuously, indifferently throwing
their burdens into the void and then returning. The dead fell
down with dangling limbs, twisted heads, open eyes and fingers spread open like flowers. Sometimes one of them traced
a scar with his heel on the layer of mushrooms, which immediately disappeared with the proliferation of the bulbs.
Then he fell head over heels into the luminous powder, falling
in slow whirls. The greenish cloud absorbed him, veiling his
fall. The interminable rain of the dead danced and fell. The
arms of the abandoned bodies made black signs in the light,
then were obliterated. Others arrived and fell. The noise of
the fall was not audible. The bodies disappeared into the pale
cloud, absorbed by the frightful sigh of the abyss.

Essaillon raised his arms. "I've seen enough. Let's go up!"
he cried.

St. Menoux, relieved, recognized, in passing, a maternity
room, penetrated the breasts of the mountain-woman, crossed
through the magma of her foetus, her growling and gloomy
intestines and finally reached the free air at the top of the
mountain.

He stopped the vibrator, breathed deeply, and joyfully
drank in the odor of the thick grass. He gave a friendly wave
of his hand to the good blue sky.

Essaillon caught his second breath. The chair's four feet
were buried in the earth.

"I wonder," said St. Menoux pensively, "what hell that hole
leads to and what horrible creatures are uttering that outcry."

"My poor friend," answered Essaillon, "can't you control
your imagination? What you call an outcry is no doubt only
the noise of a river or an underground sea. Or perhaps the
roaring of a central fire. By water or fire, the earth takes
back what it has given. As the beings of the future assimilate

all that they eat and do not emit any waste, the return of their body to dust is the only reason that the globe does not consume itself. If these men ate their dead (Why not? After all, many pagan tribes still did it in our time.), then the earth would always give and never receive. Its matter, little by little, would be entirely transformed into energy and humanity would end by moving in the bowels of a hollow planet, like a bubble which would burst one day into ether—"

"Listen!" interrupted St. Menoux. "We have been discovered."

The rumbling of the drum-chests climbed up to the earth's surface. Files of warriors streamed out of the closest cones, surrounding the mountain with a triple wall of chests, reducing to a pulp the crowd of little men that even the approach of death could not tear from their circle around the woman's stomach. The warriors began to clamber up along the abrupt slope while implanting their claws in the beaten earth.

"It's time to disappear," said Essaillon. "Let's go back down near the queen's head. I want to try an experiment."

They arrived a few moments later under the cupola's vault. Essaillon, who took too great a jump, disappeared into the mountain-being's body. St. Menoux soon saw him reappearing, his feet in the air.

"I envy your facility," said the scientist after stopping his vibrator. "For me, this ethereal locomotion is still full of surprises."

St. Menoux in turn came in contact again with the material world. His head almost touched the cupola's ceiling. His feet trampled on the red hair whose flaming waves extended several yards around the woman's face.

Through this glorious mass, he felt the soft body yielding under his feet, like an eiderdown.

"Help me get out of this chair," said the scientist. "I'm afraid that the wheels will cut her skin!"

With Peter's help, he laid on his side, unbuckled the straps and finally sat down on the hair.

"That's better," he said, out of breath. "Now, we are going

to see how the new humanity gets rid of the bodies of these immense beings when they die."

"What are you going to do?" asked a pale St. Menoux.

"Well now, we are simply going to kill this woman," replied the scientist with as much tranquillity as if he was treating a rat in the laboratory.

Out of his knapsack he drew a kitchen knife whose blade reflected flashes of blue.

"If we cut her skin, we shall likely be flooded with blood or lymph. I only see one vulnerable point—her head. I suppose that it will suffice to cut it off. Would you like to be in charge? You're more dexterous than I am."

St. Menoux suddenly sat down. The scientist's proposal had turned his legs to rubber.

"You—I—I could never do it!" he succeeding in answering. "You must not—it's murder!"

Essaillon shook his head. "You will never make a scientist if you let yourself become emotional. You have the sensitivity of a schoolteacher, my poor friend. It is not a question of murder, but an operation. By sacrificing this woman, we are amputating the new world of one of its reproductive cells which will be rapidly replaced, you can be sure. It is the disappearance of this one and the arrival of the replacement that I want to see. My, you are still very young. All right, I will operate myself."

He grasped his knife and approached the head with closed eyes, crawling on his stomach. He had great difficulty in moving. He scarcely had more than a yard to go before reaching his goal, but he had to stop several times. It took him nearly five minutes to cover the distance. Finally he straightened and sat up, waiting for his breathing to calm down. The head was exactly between his legs. He leaned over with great effort, succeeding in reaching his arms over his navel, catching the head by its hair, drawing it toward him and cutting off its head.

St. Menoux could not take his eyes from the victim's face. He saw no mark of suffering on it. The quivering corners of her mouth and her somewhat furrowed eyebrows relaxed, and the beautiful face took on an expression of serene peace.

"Just like butter," said the scientist, sighing after the effort. "No bone, no vertebral column, obviously. What would it be used for? No blood either, look!"

St. Menoux saw that the neck was without effusion of any liquid, without vein, artery or esophagus. A few nerve endings marked, here and there, her pink flesh.

"The section of this neck," said the scientist, "resembles the cooked ham that we ate yesterday at home, which reminds me that I haven't eaten anything for six hours. Fortunately, Annette thought to pack us a picnic lunch."

With a sigh of satisfaction, he took out some bread and some paté from his knapsack, holding them out to his companion. "Help yourself, my friend."

St. Menoux shook his head no. He had no appetite. He left the scientist with his meal to explore the interior of the decapitated being, its surroundings and its lower parts.

Upon his return, he found the scientist sleeping. The large man had let his untouched sandwich fall. His hands were crossed over his belly and he seemed comfortably settled. The open hood revealed his face, to which the blue light gave an appearance of marble. Some furtive waves crossed his lips, his eyelids and his smooth forehead, waves of happiness or suffering scarcely perceptible. He seemed withdrawn from the world, lost in an ineffable inner contemplation.

Peter called him, tapping him on the shoulder. Essaillon did not move. The young teacher, frightened, shook him, shouting and slapping him without effect. A flask of ammonia waved under his nostrils finally made him jump. He opened his eyes, bewildered, looked at St. Menoux without recognizing him and fell back to sleep. It was only after a quarter of an hour that Peter succeeded in waking him completely.

"I told you to be careful!" St. Menoux said reproachfully. "You let yourself be seized by the collective energy. As happened to me several times, you adopted the attitudes of the being next to you and—" He stopped short, letting his eyes rest on the woman's head resting on her hair.

The scientist blushed. "I had an extraordinary dream," he said in a quiet voice. "I will tell you about it later."

He turned his head away, trying to smile and rubbing his hands together. "Tell me, how is our patient coming along?" he asked in a strange youthful voice.

"It's extraordinary!" answered the young teacher, very happy to change the subject. "She is working like a charm! She continues to absorb the little men with her six thousand vulva and to bring large populations into the world! The decapitation you performed did not seem to bother her any more than if you had pulled out a hair."

"I'm not so surprised," remarked Essaillon. He had regained his coolness and his voice had recovered its normal tone. "In our time already, the head was the part of their body which women needed least to live! Help me to get back into my chair. We're going home."

3

Annette was gathering the last roses in the garden.

The day was coming to an end. A flame of sun remained hidden in the treetops ruffled by a light wind. A couple of doves were already looking for their evening branch. Some black martins were flying high in the fading blue sky. A gray cloud slowly stretched its rose-tinted underside toward the north. A clumsy beetle staggered along the alley gravel.

Annette raised her face toward the sky, holding a bouquet of flowers close in her arms. A thorn pricked her shoulder. She closed her eyes. The tiny pain gave her pleasure, like a tart fruit. This September day had been heavy and scorching. Its heat still oppressed her and made her heart beat heavily.

A frightful howling petrified her with horror. She recognized Peter's voice. With a great effort she threw down the roses and ran toward the laboratory, arriving there at the same time as Philomena, who was wiping her hands on her apron while running.

Annette pushed open the door, took two steps, opened her mouth to cry out and collapsed. Philomena, growling in rage, led her out of the room. St. Menoux was clutching the large marble table with two hands. He had a horrible desire to vomit. A cold sweat was running down his face and along his neck.

In front of him, on each side of the iron chair, Essaillon had fallen cut in two, from the thighs up to the cervical vertebra, as if by a gigantic thrust of a sword from bottom to top. A buttock to the left, a buttock to the right, he had slipped off each side of the chair. His head covered with the green hood remained attached to the seat, intact. Behind the large glasses the scientist's eyes opened wide and did not seem to show surprise nor suffering. His stomach had emptied on the ground in a putrid gassy puddle.

End of St. Menoux's Report

I buried my good master at the foot of a birch tree in the garden as the leaves began to fall. My heart was heavy. Dear Noel Essaillon, such a gourmand of the joys of the mind and so curious about the future. You no longer exist in the future or the past or the present. Now I suppose that you are in the position to know where this tunnel which is our lifetime opens, if I recall correctly your simile. I hope that it is in a place of infinite light where nothing remains hidden to hungry souls, like yours, wishing to know all.

Philomena and I finished the terrible job of cleaning out the laboratory. What decay there was in that man's stomach! He only ate delicate foods. Nothing but the tenderest meats, fresh vegetables and white bread made up the excrement. That is certainly one of the strangest whims of God, to burden our body with this function of transformation. Is it indeed indispensable to the universe that we are constantly passed by a current of vegetable and animal debris which decay tenderly within us?

Most men manage only to "earn their bread and keep." Yet the bread for which man toils is ultimately the earth which absorbs him.

I understand now that the new humanity sought to liberate itself from this bondage and if all is not perfect for the men of the year 100,000, the suppression of this transformation function represents considerable progress.

An examination of the remains of my good leader showed me the accident which had caused his death. When he leaned over to cut the head of the reproductive being, the seam of his diving suit split down the back, from the neck to the crotch. Neither he nor I noticed it. I did not even see it when I took him by the waist to help him into his chair. I should have seen it. I was too distracted. I will carry my remorse to my grave.

When Noel Essaillon pushed on the return button, his protective clothing left a gap about two inches wide. The part of his body which was facing this gap, no longer influenced by the noelite, remained there in the thousandth century, while the rest of him returned to 1942. The scientist returned dissected and dead. The slice remaining in the future included almost all of the spinal column and fragments of his heart, stomach, intestines and his navel.

Noel Essaillon had fallen heroically, a victim of science. I did not want his sacrifice to be in vain. I returned to the year 100,000 and finished the study of this civilization. I shall continue his manuscript from the point where death snatched it from his hands. Soon our contemporaries will know of his fantastic work and his name will be properly renown.

My first voyage after the accident led me back to the place of its occurrence. Under the cupola, in the light of the mushrooms, the debris of my master's flesh left their gloomy remnants on the golden red hair of the cut head, whose expression had not changed. The closed eyes and the finally calmed lips framed a smile of total peace. While the remains of Noel Essaillon had already partially decomposed, the head rested intact. I gathered the remains of the scientist in my sack, reached the edge of the hole of cadavers and threw my load into it.

Thus the one—thanks to whom the future is no longer an unknown—rests as he would perhaps have wanted it, both in the future and present. May he rest in peace! On Judgment Day, the pieces of his body will be reunited.

The decapitated woman continued to live. Several visits that I made afterwards found her functioning normally while her withered head took on the appearance of a hieratic mask.

I returned to the cervical rooms convinced that there existed a belt which entirely surrounded the globe. What was the role of these piles of gray matter? Did they think for the rest of the species, as we believed at first? My experiments tended to disprove this hypothesis. These heaps of brains manufactured the new energy, spreading it over the entire earth, receiving sensations and giving orders. It was entirely automatic. It was not a question of thought but of reflex.

How was this energy transmitted? How do the brain-men communicate with the others? I did not understand. Would a man from 1800 placed in front a wireless telegraph understand?

The brain-men, like the others, obeyed the supreme law which is the law of the species and of their city. It controls humanity like gravity or any other physical law. Its influence is obvious. Less evident in the twentieth century, it is still a powerful force.

What great difference exists between the circle of little men around the queen and the dance that men of our century do with contemporary women? The powerful necessity of reproduction drives them like puppets. They believe themselves free, and sing of love to both the eyes and soul of their loved ones. The law of the species leads them by the end of their sex. Tristan and Romeo were simple seedbearers. They had a mission to plant it into the soil which was awaiting them and which is always the same whether named Iseult or Juliette. The rest is literature.

My voyages to the year 100,000 and my explorations around the immense woman's womb and her six thousand identical vulvas, concealed behind six thousand forms of mirage, opened my eyes to the human condition. God willing, and with the help of my loved one, I will soon be able to find the power behind the illusion.

Annette revived from her swoon and entered a period of

delirium. Philomena treated her with herb drinks. She kept around thirty different kinds of herbs in iron boxes.

On a brisk October day, the girl rose to take her first steps since the accident. She wanted to reach the large Dagobert chair near the window which held out its solid old arms to her. The floor seemed to sink beneath her feet, the ceiling pitched, the walls began to turn, the closet replaced the window and the bed spun after the armoire. Philomena took the convalescent in her arms, sat her down with a large cushion under her feet and wrapped her in a rough wool blanket.

Annette did not dare to think and did not want to remember. She kept her mind closed. She looked at the garden veiled in a fine gray rain, almost a fog. A chestnut tree shoot had grown close to the window. Autumn had left a leaf whose five yellowed corners hung toward the ground. At times, one would deposit a drop and rise a few inches toward the sky, which overwhelmed it again with the heavy burden of drizzling rain.

St. Menoux arrived toward the end of the day. She saw him coming from the end of the alley. He descended like a drowned gray ghost in the night. Annette felt her chin tremble. Her tears added their mist to that of the rain.

Fog, rain, cold and death choked the world, crushing Annette. She was afraid; she sobbed and cried out, "Peter, Peter!" If he did not come soon, if he waited more than a second, he would no longer find her, she would surely be dead.

Peter ran to her, flinging open the door. He threw his wet overcoat on the floor. He was tall and smiling, his face golden from the strong light. He took the lost child into his arms and rocked her, kissing her eyes.

The sortilege was over. Peter closed the shutters and the curtains against the night and the water. In his arms Annette sobbed uncontrollably, trying to relieve the pain in her heart.

"We were stupid to grieve so," Peter said. "What your father had done for Philomena, we can do for him. When you are completely well, we will go and find him in the past. We shall then prevent him from taking this fatal voyage and he will avoid death."

On All Saints' Day, upon her return from mass, Philomena found her master Noel Essaillon seated in the wheelchair with his beard intact. Annette, transfigured with joy, and a smiling St. Menoux were standing next to him.

"Well, Philomena," said Essaillon in his best voice, "you seem surprised. There really is no reason to be."

"The devil! You are the devil!" murmured the maid. Her face expressed horror and fright. She made a sign of the cross on her flat chest and left the room backwards, her eyes flashing under her grey eyebrows.

St. Menoux began to laugh, but Annette had turned pale and the scientist himself seemed affected.

In the evening Annette went to the garden while her father was sleeping. Peter was waiting for her at the foot of a pine tree. They walked in the humid night, trampling the leaves. A quarter moon faded the ceiling of the clouds.

"Annie, Annette, my darling, aren't you cold?"

She pressed against him and and answered, "Near you, I shall never be cold."

They said nothing more. That was enough.

Philomena slipped out of her bed, crossing the corridor barefoot, entered the invalid's bedroom without knocking and turned on the light. Essaillon, blinking and bewildered, sat up in bed with difficulty.

"What do you want, Philomena?"

She stood before him, thin in her nightgown. Her gray hair fell in straight wisps around her face.

"I want you to go back where you came from!" she said in her peasant voice.

"What?" said the scientist, stupefied.

"And take me with you."

Essaillon shrugged his shoulders. "Come on, go to bed, my poor Philomena. You're not making sense."

She did not want to leave, she said harshly. One did not

have the right to steal the dead. When one dies, it is because
God wills it. He sets the hour. Now hell is waiting for them
both. God had punished her master by giving him a terrible
death. Since he escaped, a terrible punishment was waiting
for him for eternity. He must return to death and take with
him his poor maid overwhelmed by this stolen life.

She fell to her knees and cried. Tears ran down her old
skin. She sniffled. She was ugly.

The young couple was astonished to see the change in
Essaillon. He had lost his smile, his taste for life. He was
gloomy and began to lose weight. St. Menoux, who was
working with him on the editing of his *Essay on the Evolution
of Mankind*, found him to be distraught and absentminded.
He was disinterested in his work and wasted time in day
dreams from which he emerged with a kind of fright in his
eyes.

He had to be confined to bed. His skin hung loose and his
face was drawn. In a few days, his beard lost its sheen and
turned a sad gray color. It looked like it had been used for
a dustmop.

Philomena continued to harass him furiously. "You are still
going to die! This time your dirty inventions can do nothing
for you. You will be damned!"

She neglected the housework, waiting in the hall for op-
portunities to get the sick man alone. One heard her gnashing
her teeth and repeating the Lord's Prayer over and over
behind closed doors. She entered Essaillon's bedroom about
twenty times a day. He groaned when he saw her coming,
drawing the blankets over his head. But nothing prevented
the old harsh voice from carrying the message of fear to
his ears. When Philomena left, her words remained.

St. Menoux sent for a doctor, who diagnosed a nervous
breakdown and heart strain, complicated by uremia. The
scientist demanded the truth.

"You will not last the week," said the doctor quietly.

Essaillon threw a pillow at him, and with a furious gesture swept away the bottles which crowded his night stand. He pushed away St. Menoux, who was trying to calm him down.

When he regained his composure, he called his daughter. She sat near his bed. She tried to smile but cried instead. He looked at her a long time with passion and despair.

"Annette, my dear, I am going to leave you," he said. "Don't feel badly. We could cheat again and extend these few hours which are left to me. But I don't want to. God has manifested his will. I am going to obey."

He sighed. His eyes were set deep in his face. Philomena snarled behind the door.

A priest arrived that night. He closed himself with Essaillon and Philomena, heard their confessions and gave the sacrament of Extreme Unction to the master and the maid.

He left at dawn. In the foyer he saw St. Menoux asleep on the sofa with Annette, tiny and exhausted, huddled next to him. He nodded his head and gave them his blessing. He left the door open. The bedroom was empty.

Annette found a will on the bed that held no trace of her father's body. The scientist stated that to escape hell, he was voluntarily returning to his first death. He needed all of his courage because he was going to suffer the accident again, this time knowing what was awaiting him. He hoped that God would take the ordeal into consideration. He recommended to his daughter and St. Menoux that they never revolt against the decisions of Providence.

"Perhaps our curiosity," he added, and even the first reasons for our trips were impious. To wish to change man's condition, to try to protect them from the slightest pain, is that not going against Divine Will? We are here below to atone. The sufferings that we endure, we have personally or collectively deserved them all.

"Peter, my dear child, I am leaving you with the decision whether to continue the experiments or not. For my part, it no longer interests me. I have no other thought than to appear before God with enough humility to make me a pardon for my audacity. What are a thousand or two thousand centuries when Eternity awaits us?

"But I beseech you never to reveal the secret of the noelite, which Annette knows how to manufacture, to our unfortunate brothers. They will only use it for their torment.

"Watch over my dear daughter until she has grown up to find a husband.

"In remembrance of my poor perishable body, I am leaving you my beard. You will find it in the closet, next to the handkerchiefs."

The maid had also left a note. She apologized. She would pray for her little Annette from above. She left the address of her niece Catherine who could replace her as housekeeper.

Annette had already suffered so much pain that this new ordeal only increased her sorrow. By means of pills, she made several trips into the past to be near her living father. She found him pink and blond and optimistic, unaware of the trials which awaited him.

Relieved to know that somewhere in the past time he was still and forever happy, she spaced her visits and little by little she became accustomed to the idea of being separated from him by a distance which increased each day. She knew that she would see him again whenever she wished. She was soon satisfied with this certitude. She no longer left the present. She thought of the future. She was in love.

Part III

IMPRUDENCE

1

The year was ending. After the last two terrible winters, people looked forward to the third with apprehension. It was slow to show its anger. The housekeepers were saying, "If it could only last. We don't have enough coal. My coal dealer has not yet delivered it. And the tenant on the fourth floor has filled a full cellar of charcoal briquets for himself. Some have everything and others have nothing."

St. Menoux had given up counting the days and weeks. A calendar seemed like a ridiculous object. In the ten months which had just passed, how many centuries had he traveled through? He was snapped back to reality by poverty. He came to the end of the money that the scientist had left at his disposal. He had left the high school without warning. No doubt he was eliminated from the staff. What would he live on? What would Annette live on when he married her?

On the first death of the scientist, he had got back his room on St. James Boulevard, abandoned during the experiments for a room in the country house. In order to provide himself with the necessities, he gave a few private lessons for a meager profit. His most ignorant student, the one who paid the most, left him because of Mr. Michelet. As soon as he knew his neighbor was home, Michelet, whose senility increased each day, never failed to knock on his door to talk once more about the injustice of destiny.

St. Menoux considered moving, but he looked in vain for a cheap room. A severe lodging crisis began to rage in Paris.

He got together with the other tenants on his floor to ask Mrs. Blanet, the landlady, to throw out the old fool.

Mrs. Blanet, a widow, stayed all day in her little studio apartment, whose glass door opened on to the corridor. She interminably mended her tenants' sheets, ironed, folded and washed in the adjoining kitchen, never taking a rest.

She rarely smiled. She regretted not being able to do everything. After her husband's death, she had been forced to engage a maid. This expense caused her great sorrow, which often changed to anger at the expense of the unfortunate asthmatic and lame scullion whom she worked like a locomotive, or at the dogs of the neighborhood, who persisted on urinating under her window.

She received the delegation in her usual outfit, a mauve peignoir which wrapped around her fleshy body and whose hem, elbows and big bust were filthy gray. She refused to throw out a man who paid regularly and whose conversation she appreciated.

"I do not see what you find wrong with him," she said. "He is a man of education. It would be very unkind on my part to send him away."

St. Menoux had to give up giving lessons in his room. He went out to the homes. The subway was time consuming. Meals in restaurants were horribly expensive and left him hungry. Miss Mongent, who lived on the fourth floor, offered him a ration card for seven dollars. Miss Mongent worked at the town hall. She slipped false cards into the files and sold the good ones to her clients.

Peter bought a pound of butter from the coal merchant. It cost a dollar. "That's not expensive," said the man. "In Neuilly, they are paying up to a dollar and a half." He bought some Camembert cheese from the hairdresser for twenty cents and from the milkman, a pair of stockings for sixty cents which he exchanged at the bakery for a pound of smoked beef.

In this way he fed himself at home for a while. His

scruples forced him to refuse almost all of Annette's invitations. He saw her less and less, monopolized by his lessons and despairing of finding a way to offer her a suitable existence. Perhaps her father had left her a great deal of money. That was one more reason he had to be able to assure her a comfortable future.

On the day when he changed his last twenty dollar bill, the idea came to him to put on the diving suit again, which he had not touched since Essaillon's final death, and to use it to get money. The vibrator would allow him to enter safes and relieve them of their contents. For a moment, he entertained the idea of retrieving a little of the gold of the Bank of France held in the Martinique. But he had the education of an honest man and his conscience kept whispering the word robbery. He could not cross the moral barrier which forbade such access to affluence.

It seemed to him, though, that he would be less guilty if he operated outside of the present time. It was useless to go into the future to collect bills which did not yet exist, but rather into the past, which was full of resources. The past was only shadows and memories. To steal from a shadow, to plunder a memory, was that really stealing?

After a three-day debate, pressed by necessity, he answered himself, "No." and planned his first experiment. He told Annette of his intentions. She watched him talking. She trembled at the sound of his voice. She paid little attention to the meaning of the words. He could do no wrong.

As the goal of his voyage, he chose the year 1890. To him, this epoch seemed bathed in a golden light and famed for its abundance of gold coins.

At the moment of departure, he thought of piles of coins, swollen sacks and full strongboxes. But he found himself on arrival seated on the knees of the beautiful tart Suzanne, who was on her way to the milliner, in an uncovered coach pulled by four horses, accompanied by her lover, the Baron of Bois de l'Orme.

The beautiful Suzanne uttered a frightened cry and fainted at this apparition. The Baron stood up trembling, but his old knees gave way. He fell to his seat and began to stammer. His teeth began to chatter. The two footmen dressed in red who were standing behind the coach, raised their arms to the sky, falling backwards. The coachman turned around, opened his mouth wide, whipped his horses, then stopped them, jumped to the ground and fled. The horses peacefully trotted across the causeway and Faubourg St. Honoré Street was jammed in a wink.

St. Menoux looked with interest at the beautiful, limp woman, clothed in a long bell skirt in pale blue satin which rose up to her breast and a bodice of white tulle with puffed sleeves and a high neck. A bow of royal blue velvet trimmed the waist. A ribbon of the same velvet passed under her chin and held a headdress, half-hat, half-bonnet, of ruffled pale blue tulle, from which thousands of blond curls escaped.

Her head was resting on her shoulder. She opened one eye slightly and closed it immediately. She had a very tiny mouth, a turned-up nose and a solid, business woman's chin.

St. Menoux found her charming. He smiled and began ridding her of her handbag, her diamond bracelet and a few small rings. The Baron tried to gather his courage. With one blow, St. Menoux sat him down. His top hat fell off, dragging his wig along with it. He had a pink spot in the middle of his skull.

Horrified women leaned out the windows, splitting their corsets, pointing out the robber and calling for help. The entire studio of Rosandrée, a great seamstress, screamed from the windows. The foreman, Julia, a tall brunette, lost her chignon. Her hair flowed to the mezzanine. The coach horses were prancing, the horseshoes were clacking, the whips cracking, the coachmen swearing and the pedestrians crowding.

Two heavy policemen rushed toward him. One dragoon

lieutenant with a blond moustache, handsome as a rainbow, leaped on the coach step. But when he put his hand out, the offender disappeared. The entire street cried out. In less than a minute there were twenty different descriptions of the bandit, his arrival and his departure. Mrs. Lurin, a milliner, carrying two round hatboxes; the small flour-covered pastry cook Gaston, with his flat basket on his head; the wet nurse Adelaide, who was walking two twins in a wicker carriage beribboned in pink; Ferdinand the traveling photographer, crushed under the weight of his camera, tripod, and his moustache, and 427 other persons hastened toward their clients, their parents or their friends to bring them the astonishing news.

The gallant officer helped the Baron to the sidewalk, revived the beautiful woman and saw her home. The policemen arrived when everything was over. Two policemen in round hats, ugly as seals, led away Odette, a prostitute whose presence in this bourgeois district was quite a scandal.

St. Menoux walked up the boulevards and Royal Street. The sight of the street delighted him. Plump little women were toddling along and smiling. Their pointed shoulders, their slender waists, their hats perched on top of their high hairdos all added to their gay and perky silhouettes. Those who wanted to walk faster lifted their skirts, showing their ankles. Men with opera hats and narrow pants turned around to catch this sight while straightening out their moustaches.

The pedestrians walked both in the road and on the sidewalk. They scarcely bothered to get out of the way of the slow-moving coaches. The coachmen yelled out spicy compliments to the ladies and friendly insults to the men. Carriages of lords, polished like old furniture, rolled fast behind pairs of matched horses, whose buttocks were as round as the ladies'. Dung heaps reeked in the streets.

Those are happy people, the traveler said to himself. I went far into the future to seek happiness which was, in truth, behind me.

For a few moments he forgot the selfish goal of his expedition and began to explore the capital. He soon changed his mind about the happiness of the city. In the bourgeois districts he found an instability and a futility that lowered men to the level of women. They preoccupied themselves with styles, horses, theater and spoke stereotyped witticisms. The eternal dramas of adultery filtered through apartments overloaded with furniture and veiled with several thicknesses of curtains.

In the workers' districts there was great misery. Growing industry had begun to crush labor. As St. Menoux was passing through a gloomy room, he stopped. Death rattles filled his ears. He slipped onto a bed and saw a couple on a ripped mattress dying with open mouths. Four half-naked children struggled feebly on a layer of rags slimy with filth thrown on the floor. A charcoal stove glowed in a corner of the bedroom, pouring a dull poison out into the somber air.

The haggard mother, lying on the edge of the bed, watched death come closer and closer to her children. Her large frightened eyes reflected the small pink light of the stove. Her bony shoulder stuck out of her torn shirt. Her hair fell in straggly strands over the edge of the mattress. Her weak arms hung over the bed and her fingertips touched the head of the youngest and most loved child. He had just stopped breathing. His little gray arms rested next to his calm body. The eldest daughter, near the wall, was trying to catch her breath, tearing at her rags and revealing her throat withered from starvation. Beside her a boy was crying. She took him into her arms, then let him go. She was slipping away.

The calm father, stretched out on his back and thin as a dead bird, was looking at the cracked ceiling, breathing the dirty air, feeling hunger and everyday horror. He was finally dead, finished.

St. Menoux almost obeyed his first reflex, to open the door and window and let in some fresh air, throw out the coalstove and save these miserable people. But the window faced the

back of a greenish courtyard and the door faced a black
corridor.

He slowly walked through the deadly vapors, floated above
the limp bodies. He took a large jump and rose straight up
toward the blue sky, through the ramshackle floors, rickety
furniture, wine-filled arguments and empty plates. He did not
have the right to rescue these miserable beings.

Besides, all that is only memory, he thought. These people
have been dead for fifty years.

He shook himself and promised never to let himself become
emotionally involved in these sights which, after all, were
fifty years old. He decided to immediately begin serious
work.

Bathing in the blue sky and washing away the odors of
misery that he had just passed through, he plunged toward
a street next to the Stock Exchange. He entered a large bank.
The bald teller was arranging sacks of gold coins in the
strongbox. St. Menoux slipped through the railing and waited
for the man to be called to the window. He then stopped the
vibrator and put the sacks from the safe into his knapsacks.

The teller suddenly saw his client open his mouth, open
his eyes wide and take on the bewildered face of a child who
sees a giraffe for the first time. This man was looking at
something which was happening in his safe, behind him. He
turned around and recognized in terror that one of the two
nightmares which had haunted his nights for thirty years had
just come true.

The first of these dreams found him responsible for a large
error. He was always making mistakes. He gave ten gold
coins too many for each deposit. He knew it but continued to
make mistakes. He recounted his piles. He counted ten but
knew that there were eleven. So the blood of the safe and
his own blood went drop by drop into the hands of his
lively clients—joyful vampires who filed rapidly in front of his
teller's cage.

The second nightmare was of a diabolical thief who defied
locks and surveillance and burglarized his safe right under

his nose. Paralyzed, he could not prevent him from taking the beautiful plump sacks. Sweat ran down his forehead. He wailed and cried. The thief sneered, devouring the gold coins like candy and left with the stomach of a pregnant woman.

The two dreams always finished in the same way. The manager held back from the guilty teller half of his $12.50 salary until the end of his career and made him stand before a criminal court after firing him.

Only a nightmare could admit such a calamity. He used to wake up in the middle of the night, first trembling and then overcome with joy at realizing that they were only dreams. When he took advantage of this nocturnal awakening to go to the bathroom, his wife in curlers would turn over and groan, "You ate too much soup again."

The impossibility of this man's presence in his safe reassured him. He said to himself, "You are dreaming again." But since this statement did not awaken him, he knew that he was not sleeping and began to tremble. The other moustached employers were already standing around the railings and yelling. About twenty clients pushed their faces against the teller's cage. The teller reassured himself. I don't know how he entered, he said to himself, but he will never get out. He recovered his voice and yelled, "Guard the door! I'll hold him."

He opened a drawer, aimed a revolver at the thief and advancing bravely, seized his left wrist. With the other hand he pointed the weapon at his chest.

"Surrender!" he cried.

His hand closed on nothingness, and his nails gripped his own palm. The thief had disappeared.

"Ah!" sighed the teller with relief, "it was a dream after all." But the sight of the empty safe filled him with new horror. He probed inside. He felt it cold, solid and real. His entire life's salary could not reimburse what had just disappeared. He pressed the revolver against his temple. He had read in novels how broken bankers shoot themselves in the head. His revolver was large and his head very small.

The bullet went through him without difficulty and buried itself in the ceiling, after piercing the gas pipe which whistled
like a tea kettle.

That evening St. Menoux went to the opera. *Faust* was
being presented as a benefit performance for the benefit of a
missionary project which was buying back young Chinese.

Old Faust interrogated nature and the Creator in vain,
before the total indifference of the audience. They had come
to show themselves off. The most beautiful shoulders of Paris
were there. The men leered at the daring décolletages. Ladies'
lorgnettes were pointed not toward the stage but rather toward the loges or the first row in the orchestra.

A crash in the orchestra—Faust at the end beckoned Mephistopheles. Sensational! Novelty! Boldness! Two devils appeared at the same time on the stage, a red one to the
left and a green one to the right. The room applauded. The
stage manager, between two stage props, insulted the intruder
with wild gestures and soundless words. The orchestra leader,
baffled for a moment, began again to conduct. The green
devil disappeared as he came. Bravo! Very good! Charming! The trick was very successful. No one knew what it
meant and they didn't ask questions. The spectators who were
present never took the trouble to figure it out. They would
read in tomorrow's newspaper what they should already have
known.

When the noise abated, Faust renewed his dialogue with
the real Mephistopheles, whose name was Bernard and who
suffered from rheumatic fever.

A loud cry interrupted their exchange of compliments. The
green devil surged like a flame into the Grande Duchess of
Berindol's box. She was a dowager rather well preserved for
her seventy years of intelligent debauchery. Her old leather
skin had rubbed against a number of bodies, smooth and
hairy—princes, workmen, strong soldiers, perfumed cardinals,
dirty artists and little shepherds who smelled of cheese.
Only the devil was missing from her collection. She shuddered

when she saw him stretch out his green hands toward her. But he only wanted her diamond necklace. She tried to claw him but her hands struck a void.

The entire audience stood up. Ten officers rushed toward the Grande Duchess who bombarded them with epithets. Mephistopheles took advantage of the public's inattention to rub his knees. An outcry rose from the room. The green phantom had just reappeared in the loge of Mr. Fortoni of Fortoni wines. The inventor of the famous restorative never went out without a sample of his elixir, which all the famous European courts had tasted. Trembling, he pulled out a flat flask from his pocket and held it out to the apparition, who smashed it on his bald head. He fell back into his seat and allowed the thief to strip him of his diamond shirt buttons and cuff links. He also watched his aggressor seize the five-strand pearl necklace from his wife's fat neck.

Some courageous men burst in the loge door. The thief jumped over the balcony. The crowd gave chase, screaming, but he disappeared in the middle of his trajectory and vanished somewhere between the balcony and the back of a chair. Panic gripped the audience. Forty women fainted. Others ran screaming toward the exits, pushing and clawing. The men pushed harder than the women, trampling over the fallen ones, disheveling their hairdos, tearing at their dresses and clinging to their corset strings.

Although the doors were jammed by the panic, a few people succeeded in getting out. Staggering, they descended the large stairway with their arms outstretched like blind men. They ran away faltering and disappeared into the night, leaving only a flickering sad, green lamp post light.

After several similar expeditions St. Menoux had gathered a veritable pirate's treasure—three chests of jewels, gold pieces and spoons. His future was assured.

One afternoon, after returning from a new foray, he re-

alized that he had run out of space to store his booty. He
decided that he had collected enough and that nothing now
stood in the way of his marriage to Annette. He strolled
through Paris. The warming month of March radiated mild-
ness and a soft light. Along the quays, the trees outstretched
their lacy branches, dotted with buds, toward a pale sky
as blue as a dreamy girl's eyes. The chubby sparrows barely
moved at the sound of his footsteps. The slow water of the
Seine carried a barge downstream. Beyond the Double
Bridge, Notre Dame loomed with all its beauty in a light
haze, looking to St. Menoux exactly as he had seen it fifty-
three years and two hours earlier. The stone profile, slightly
darker, stood out against a mild sky.

If the scenery had not changed the men, on the contrary,
exhibited a painful transformation. In the sweet early spring
air, they walked with worried faces, hunched backs and wan
eyes.

St. Menoux had to recall the smiles of the 1890 crowd
to appreciate the wry faces of 1943. He wondered at the
irritated looks of the people in the automobile era. Women
rushed around him, hardly looking at each other, each engrossed with her own particular problem.

Peter closed his eyes and recalled the graceful images of
the time that he had just explored. He thought that it would
be fun to bring Annette there for a honeymoon. If she liked
it, nothing would prevent them from settling there for eternity. Although it was uncomfortable for the young teacher
to think of living off the fortune of others. But now he had
enough money to establish his own fortune.

Instinctively he rummaged through a book-dealer's stand.
A title caught his eye: *The Mystery of the Green Devil.* He
flipped through the old yellow-paged book. He had barely
read two pages before he handed a dollar to the vendor.
Running to the nearest cafe, he continued to read. It was the
story of his own appearances in the 1890's, narrated by an
author of the period. One sketch represented him three

times larger than life, with glasses large as automobile head-lights, strangling the Grande Duchess of Berindol.

"Idiot!" cried the head waitress to her brat who was crawl-ing under the tables. "If you tear your pants again, I'll hand you over to the Green Devil!"

St. Menoux spent seven afternoons in the library. He found more than six hundred books devoted to the Green Devil. Journalists, scientists, doctors and criminologists sought to solve the mystery of these sudden appearances and thefts. Some spoke of black magic, while others indicted an orga-nized gang. Freemasonry, Jesuits, or the Black Hand were blamed. The young teacher realized that the Green Devil was more notorius than the beast of Gevaudun, Mandrin, Croquemitaine or Cartouche, and that he was an important figure in popular folklore. All unsolved murders in 1890 were blamed on him, as well as a few disappearances and kid-nappings. It was he who had sent the trunk to Goufe; he who fed the faster of Puy, who claimed not to have eaten for six years; he who burst the hot air balloon of the Chaptal brothers when it reached an altitude of fifteen thousand feet. It was he who instigated the May revolutions; he who almost threw President Sadi-Carnot overboard during his visit to the Toulon Squadron; he who ruined the apple cider crop in Normandy and he who induced the rains which flooded seven districts of southern France.

One royalist author claimed that the Green Devil was a famous personality of the Republic in disguise. This explained his immunity. The archbishop of Paris went to exorcize, with great ceremony, a convent whose nuns saw a pink devil with a red head under their beds each night. An actress of the French Theater claimed to have been raped by him, and for three weeks all of France waited for the news bulletin which would reveal the sequel to this spree. The date passed. No more doubt. She was pregnant by the Green Devil! Her spouse fainted while playing in a Musset play and vomited in the arms of a stagehand. Three gynecologists came to examine her. It was her menopause.

Finally, St. Menoux was aghast when he saw in the *Mathematics Review* an article under his own signature entitled, "The geometric progression in group hallucination and rumor: The case of the Green Devil." It was in the volume of November 1938. He remembered having published a study on the number "three" in this volume. He went home and consulted his collection. He also found an article on the Green Devil. The article on "three" had disappeared! He read the article devoted to group hallucination and found it very well written. He tried to remember what he had written on the number three, but it was very vague in his mind. On the contrary, he began to remember having written the study on hallucination.

He shook himself, plunged his face in cold water and tried to distinguish his old memories from his new ones. However, the old ones gradually vanished.

He decided to visit Annette. Her smile, the warmth of her arms would return his sanity. She was as natural and simple as flowers. Next to her nothing seemed complicated nor difficult. Confusing probabilities disappeared. Only the essential remained.

She held out her open hands to him and said, "I've been waiting for you."

She had waited patiently for him every hour of her life. She said to herself, "I am his fiancée. He will come." She would sit by the window and look at the trees behind which he lived, somewhere in the far distance.

He sat at her feet. His long folded legs pointed their knees to the left and right. He took Annette's soft hands in his dry ones and kissed her fingers one at a time. He then cupped her hand and placed his forehead in it. His Adam's apple rose and descended along his neck. He sighed and placed his head on her knees. What was he looking for? He was happy.

St. Menoux came to this conclusion: his interventions in the past had changed the entire era which separated this past from the present. The Green Devil, created within a few weeks by his journeys into the lost century, had conquered fifty years in the memory of the world.

The young teacher was overcome by his discovery. He resolved to attempt a new experiment, following the rigorous laws of scientific research. In the National Library, he had a work by the monk, Chamayou, of the French Academy, photographed page by page. It was an honest piece of work. The author enumerated all of the appearances of the Green Devil for which he had found at least four witnesses, devoting a chapter to each one. St. Menoux took two sets of photos from each page, stamped with the seal of the National Library. He kept one set at home and left his hotel to lock the other set in one of the noelite safes at Essaillon's villa, where, on the way, he bumped into Mr. Michelet on the sidewalk.

The architect seized him by the arm. "Ah, Mr. St. Menoux," he said. "How happy I am to see you!" He was sniffling. His neck floated in his dirty detachable collar. His goatee had shed on his vest.

"Mr. St. Menoux," he continued. "Pardon my asking this favor of you, but today is the eighth of the month and I have no bread ticket for the next two weeks. Could you lend me a pound or two? Everything is so expensive. I eat almost nothing but bread and never have enough of it."

He wiped his eyes with his thumb, sniffling. "To be reduced to begging! Do you think that is proud? What would my parents say if they were still living? Just think, Mr. St. Menoux, they were married at the Madeleine Church."

St. Menoux snapped out of his dream and looked at the architect. He had grown thin; he had aged by twenty years. His clothes were falling off him. Compassionate but harried, St. Menoux gave him half of his bread ticket and hurried on his way. He had barely turned his back when Mr. Michelet entered the Bougnat Bar and gave the owner the fruit of his begging. The man from Auvergne bought his tickets at the price of five pounds against a coffee cup of prewar liquor.

It was the unconcious memory of this meeting that determined the direction of the new voyage that St. Menoux undertook. He wanted to rob a jeweler on the Rue de la Paix and see if this new exploit would be recorded and pictured in Canon Chamayou's book. When he left, he was thinking of a jeweler's shop that he had seen during his previous explorations. But his subconscious led him to a marriage room in the town hall of the Eleventh District. He arrived there as the mayor, in a black robe and beard, was asking the bride the usual question: "Miss Angela Martin-Marin, do you accept Mr. Anselm Michelet as your lawful husband?"

The young woman, very moved, raised her veiled head to answer "Yes," when through the netting she saw instead of the mayor, the Green Devil. She stood petrified with her mouth opened wide. The apparition said to her fiance, "So you are Mr. Michelet. I've known your son well."

St. Menoux found the future bride a bit thin, but touching in her pallor. Without waiting he exited through the walls.

The jewelry he was eying belonged to Mr. Gaston Poulet, one of the most famous experts on precious stones in the world. At his counter the jeweler was examining five magnificent diamonds, which a broker from Pretoria was showing him. Mr. Poulet was nearing sixty. His thinning hair, pasted down on both sides of his center part, and his handlebar moustache were an unnatural black. He sighed with pleasure. This eighteen carat diamond was a perfect marvel! He unscrewed his magnifying glass from its socket and set the stone down.

"I will buy the lot," he said to the South African.

At that exact moment, there was a slight stirring in the

air near the two men. An enormous green hand slipped between them, moving in a half-curl onto the tray and closing around the diamonds.

"The Green Devil!" stammered Mr. Poulet. Mr. William Dubington had just arrived from London. He had never heard of this devil. He saw only a common thief. A traveling salesman of valuable merchandise, he never ventured out without arms. From his adolescence as a wharf porter at the Cape, he had kept his brutal manners and contempt for firearms. He drew a large knife from his vest and plunged it at St. Menoux's stomach. St. Menoux jumped backward, avoiding sudden death. But the point of the knife cut his diving suit from top to bottom, about ten inches, and slightly scratched his flesh up to his navel.

He grew pale from fright. It was a catastrophe! He could use neither the vibrator nor the return button before repairing the suit, without suffering the same fate as his unfortunate partner. He rushed toward the door with the hope of reaching a deserted corner where he could proceed with the mending. The African ran after him, shouting, "Thief!" in every language.

The "Devil" ran down the avenue of the Opera, followed by a dark-skinned fanatic who was baying like a dog and provoking a great sensation. Coachmen whipped their horses and women pulled their skirts up to their knees to run faster. Dogs began to yelp and the more courageous men joined the pursuit. Jacket lapels flew in the wind and opera hats rolled on the pavement. St. Menoux ran toward the Opera, searching in vain for a deserted place. Alerted by the news, merchants and innkeepers, with round hats and brooms in their hands, rushed to their doors. St. Menoux saw to his horror, the entire city population. He could see no escape.

He was running out of breath. The pack grew behind him. Children and dogs joined the men and the entire avenue shouted, "It's the Green Devil. Green Devil! Green Devil!"

A black coach harnessed to a drooping horse was parked along the sidewalk.

St. Menoux jumped on the stepladder, shouted "Boo!" to the coachman, who fainted with fright on the other side of the seat, and woke the horse with a sharp blow of the whip. The beast took off in a gallop. In a roar of grating iron and wood, the coach bounded down the street. Two, five, ten coaches launched out in pursuit. St. Menoux knew how to control a cab but not a horse. Instinctively the horse turned the corner of the Opera Square and stampeded toward the Madeleine Church. On Royal Street there were about fifty pursuers. Like a hurricane, open carriages, baby carriages, coupes, cabs and phaetons all sped on, hooking together, turning over, climbing the sidewalks, flattening garbage cans, tearing up lamp posts, pulverizing storefronts and crushing small children.

One four-wheeled carriage roared into a pastry shop, the disemboweled horse scattering his innards over the tarts.

At the end of the band was a carriage carrying a tipsy honeymoon couple. The rosy bride brandished her bouquet and shouted between hiccups, "To death!"

St. Menoux's coach took the curve on one wheel and rushed down Rivoli street. The mass of pursuers whirled around Concord Square. The African, astride a broken down nag drawing only two broken shafts of a cart, led the pursuit, heading a tornado of galloping feet, reeking buttocks, bounding wheels, cracking frames, snapping horseshoes, splitting wood, cracking whips and epithets.

In the wake of the chase, the deserted street was scattered with debris—dead horses with their feet in the air and sprawled women with petticoat lace aflutter.

St. Menoux's horse wanted to turn down Pyramide Square. Carried away by a gigantic bound, he collided with the pillar of an arcade. The coach wheels flew off to the sides. Mr. William Dubington found the thief unconscious in the middle of the debris. His first impulse was to search the haversacks.

He recovered his diamonds and left. The whole affair did not interest him any longer.

Pain awoke St. Menoux faster than the best attendant could have. He found himself on a cell bench. In order to put on a straitjacket, they had stripped him of his diving suit.

2

When he left for the other periods, Peter had always told Annette about how long he'd be gone. Annette used to go to the laboratory well in advance of his return. She understood best the principle and operation of the apparatus. Yet this scientific research, rather than corrupting her mind, had kept her open to wonder. When her fiancé suddenly appeared before her eyes, she would feel the same joyful surprise each time.

More than the moment of his return, perhaps, she enjoyed those moments that preceded it. Alone in the empty room, standing before the exact spot where he was to return, her hands clasped to prevent her from trembling with emotion, she would look at the void, listening to the silence and trying to catch the distant sound of the traveler approaching through the years. She would hear nothing but the tremors and the deafening tumult of her own body. Then suddenly, looming from nothingness, he would be there, so large and thin, twisted and bent, and clothed entirely in green. Taking her eyes from the chameleon, she would smile and hold out her arms to him. She would abandon herself to him, choked with happiness.

Today she waited in vain. At the end of an hour, her eyes hollowed, irritated from impatience, she began to imagine the worst possible misfortunes. She waited all evening and all night. Catherine could not tear her away from her vigil. Catherine, Philomena's niece, had left her Normandy farm and her lover to obey her aunt's last wish. She understood her mistress' pain.

She was a solid twenty-five-year-old blonde with a full bosom and round blue eyes. As a result of carrying her eleven little brothers and sisters on her right arm, one after the other, while attending to the household chores, she remained inclined to the left and walked somewhat askew. She spent the night with Annette, where, seated in an armchair, she fell asleep. Annette paced the floor, bit her fingernails in anguish and shook the maid to ask her to listen with her.

At dawn she fell into deep despair. She did not want to leave the laboratory. Catherine had to set up a cot for her in the corner and make her drink a potion of poppies which barely succeeded in putting her to sleep for two hours.

When she awoke, an idea came to her. She jumped out of bed and ran to the iron vault where her father's diving suit was locked. She found a pair of scissors, a needle and thread, and reduced it to her size. Dipping it in a fresh bath of noelite, she put it on without even waiting for it to dry. Since some accident must be preventing Peter from returning to her, she would go to join him. She filled the knapsacks with provisions, medication and adhesive material soaked in noelite.

He needed help. "I'm coming, my love! Don't be afraid. I'm here. I'm coming!" she cried to him across time. She rushed her final preparations, buckling the belt, kissing a trembling Catherine. At the moment of adjusting the slide index, she suddenly began to cry. She knew that Peter had left for 1890. But he had not told her the month, day or hour. Without unbelievable luck she would never find him.

The police found some strange objects in the Green Devil's pockets. First, a soldier's book attesting that he was born in 1910 and that he had gone to war against Germany in 1939. One letter bore some stamps of the French state, with the likeness of an unknown old man. Also found were some colored sheets of paper, divided into small numbered squares on which were imprinted the words "bread" "potatoes" "meat" and this strange phrase: "miscellaneous." Finally a newspaper dated July 11, 1943. Composed of a single sheet, it was entirely dedicated to the war of Germany against Russia. One photograph, reproduced by a perfected process, illustrated two monstrous engines—mobile bastions of steel, armed with cannons aimed to attack.

The examining magistrate, Mr. Vigne, shuddered while looking at this picture. "A nation," he muttered to himself, "which possessed a dozen such machines would rule the world!" He turned the page. Another photograph showed two men in a flying apparatus with stretched wings. Beside it, a four-line article announced that the Parisians were going to exchange a pound of turnips for the DZ ticket.

Evening Paris, mused Mr. Vigne. A strange title. This method of illustration was very curious. One would say photographs. Millions of dead . . . bombardment of cities . . . twenty-five ships sent to the Arctic Ocean . . . the Japanese at the door of Australia . . . Vichy government . . . one gallon of wine per week. Surely he is crazy. A genius perhaps, but a madman. He is delirious.

Before passing the death sentence, he decided to interrogate the prisoner once more, out of curiosity rather than necessity. The conviction was final. Mr. Vigne, an honest civil servant, was reaching fifty. He possessed the arthritic temperament which causes a bony forehead, sickly, fine blond hair, a receding hairline and protruding teeth under a thin moustache. He made St. Menoux sit down between four guards and began the cross-examination.

Peter was overcome by the stupidity of his misadventure. Here he was, a prisoner of the past, enchained by shadows! The four brutes who were watching him with stubborn faces were no more than memory and decay, and he, the scientist with the cunning body, found himself stupidly arrested during his voyage by these backward phantoms. He felt the entire weight of their ignorance, felt their incredulity and the complete improbability of his situation.

If he told the truth, no one would believe his story. If he invented lies, he would only aggravate his case before this outdated court of justice.

He barely listened to the magistrate's first questions, and finished by stating that he would only answer before the two members of the Science Academy.

"My case is not answerable to justice," he said, "but to the laws of physics and chemistry. Besides, my papers are on your desk. You can see perfectly clearly that I am not your contemporary! A half century separates us."

"Certainly, certainly," said the judge in a soft voice. "We know. Don't get upset. Can you tell me what strange idea induced you to put on this green costume for your robberies?"

St. Menoux, his heart racing, saw the magistrate rise and take out from a wall cupboard a package which he untied. As Mr. Vigne laid it out on his desk, he recognized the gloves, the boots, the haversack, the earphones, the glasses (miraculously intact) and finally the belt and the controls which the judge placed on top of everything, and which did not seem to have suffered any damage.

A mad hope rose in the young teacher's heart. His manacled hands trembled on his knees when he answered, "I—I can only explain it to you with a direct demonstration. For that you must allow me to put it on for a few minutes.

Mr. Vigne shook his head. "So that you can play another one of your tricks? Not that I believe a word of your so-called 'disappearances.' They are the gossip of excited crowds. But I consider you a very crafty criminal and I do not plan to give you an opportunity to demonstrate your talents. First of all, give me an explanation. I will then decide if a demonstration is necessary."

"Well, here goes," said St. Menoux. He swallowed his saliva and gave the first explanation that came to his mind.

"It is a bulletproof vest."

"Ah really," sneered Mr. Vigne. "Bulletproof? And knife proof too, I suppose?"

"I mean—"groaned St. Menoux, abashed.

"You mean that you are trying to lie to me!" shouted Mr. Vigne, beating his fist on the desk. "I demand the truth. No stories. And what does this mechanism and these buttons and these regulators mean? Perhaps you tell me that it is a coffee mill? Besides, I shall see for myself."

He stretched out his right hand toward the controls. St. Menoux jumped to his feet, shouting, "No, don't!"

The four guards rushed him and threw him back into his chair. A hairy hand covered his mouth. His eyes popping out of his sockets, he saw the magistrate's index finger move for a moment across the three buttons, hesitate, and then chose with a sharp thrust the middle one.

"Oh!" exclaimed Mr. Vigne.

"What?" cried the four guards.

St. Menoux fell unconscious.

On the desk there remained no trace of the skin of the Green Devil.

Annette had just lived through the fourth day of her helpless vigil. She hardly ate. Locked in the laboratory, she watched for the invisible. She tried to hear the stirrings of silence, to sense the breath of air, to imagine, in the void of the room, the transparent form of her lover. She told herself that perhaps he was there, separated from her by an instant in time, by a thousandth of a second, more insurmountable than a fortress wall. She sometimes rose from her chair, searching for a phantom with her trembling hands.

She finally gave in to fatigue, falling asleep for a few minutes and then awakening with a start, sure that her momentary weakness had made her miss the opportunity of joining or saving Peter. Remorse added to her anguish.

Once more she had let herself fall asleep when a slight noise awoke her. With puzzled eyes she saw a dark bundle on the ground between the two marble tables on the very spot

where Peter should have appeared. She rushed to it and recognized the diving suit and its accessories. She pressed them
to her heart, sobbing.

"Catherine!" she called out. "Catherine, hurry!"

"You see? You see?" she said to the running maid. She
held out the green remains in her arms, sobbing. They cautiously unfolded the pieces of the suit and laid them out
on the table. When Annette looked at the tear in the stomach,
she clenched her hands.

"My God, there's blood," said Catherine, pointing to a
spot.

Annette moaned and caressed the cut material, tears falling
on to her hands.

"My Peter, my darling, my little one. Where are you? Are
you in pain? Tell me, Peter, my love—" Suddenly she stood
up straight. "My God!" she said. "Why didn't I think of it
sooner?"

She took the apparatus which had returned with the diving
suit. The very fact that it came back proved that it was
functioning. And the position of the index on the regulator
told her exactly at what place in time St. Menoux could be
found.

The weight of death lifted from her chest. Now she would
be able to join him and save him. She glued a band of
material to the tear in the outfit and filled the knapsacks
with all of the necessary provisions for an expedition. She
put on her diving suit, put the other one in her sack, and
regulated her own controls according to St. Menoux's.

In less than ten minutes, she was ready to leave.

Mr. Vigne believed what he saw. He was forced to believe
in a miracle. He tried to get an explanation from his prisoner,
who had regained consciousness after several vigorous slaps
by the police. But St. Menoux no longer noticed his surroundings. His lone hope of rejoining his century one day had
just vanished. It did not matter what they did to him now.

The judge left his desk and walked back and forth in front

of the prisoner. He was flushed with confusion. He felt both ashamed of his ignorance before this supernatural phenomenon and vexation at not being able to deny it. He stopped abruptly, leaned toward the prisoner and asked him questions which even he knew were stupid. This made him blush even more.

St. Menoux did not reply or even look at him. He was crushed with despair. This century, which had seemed to him so full of charm when he walked in it before returning to his own, now seemed as strange, as ferocious and as backward as the age of the cavemen. And even more grotesque, with its mustaches and crumb-catching beards.

The brutal epoch from which he now found himself forever separated was the only one worth being lived in by men of mature minds. It was a serious era. No one lost time there. No one amused himself.

Then too, it contained Annette. St. Menoux was suddenly overwhelmed with pain. Tears flowed down his cheeks. Mr. Vigne knitted his brows.

Peter would never see his sweet fiancée again. He closed his eyes and imagined her hair, fresh as spring, and the purity of her glance, so overwhelming with its confidence and its gift of self. His heart swelled and filled his entire chest. He cried, "Annette."

"Peter, my darling, I am here," she answered.

St. Menoux jumped to his feet.

"What?" said the four guards.

"Oh, an accomplice," said Mr. Vigne. "Seize him!"

The guards rushed forward, clutching the air, their lowered heads crashing into each other.

The carriage which brought the Green Devil from the Palace of Justice to the prison also carried a transparent girl, who did not think for a second of looking at the sight, new for her, of this quaint Paris, because nothing in the world's past, present, or future was as beautiful as her beloved's face.

One hour later, with all the force of her love, she knocked

out the guard who had been locked in the cell for pre-
cautionary measure and flew away with St. Menoux, through
the walls of space and time.

"Hurry up and come to eat!" shouted Catherine. "Don't
you know that the curfew is at eight o'clock this evening?"

The curfew! St. Menoux began to laugh. This world
seemed magnificent to him. Ah, 1943! He wanted black bread
this evening, and he refused butter for his noodles. Ah, the
wonderful era of restrictions!

He drew his little Annette very close to his heart. He
swore to himself never again to put himself in a situation
where he would run the risk of never seeing her again. Then
he went on his way to the subway, smiling at the ill-tempered
people who pushed aginst him. He arrived at his hotel, per-
spiring, at 7:58 P.M. In his room the memory of his appearance at the town hall of the Eleventh District returned
to mind. "I shall tell the good Mr. Michelet that his mother
was a very beautiful bride." He knocked on his neighbor's
door.

"Come in," shouted a woman's voice.

Surprised, he pushed open the swinging door. He saw an
unmade bed, a table covered with dirty linen and rags on
top of which a cat was curled up, asleep. Seated on a low
chair, an old woman with yellow hair was looking at him.
Her feet were soaking in a basin.

"Oh, excuse me. I knocked on the wrong door."

"No harm, Mr. St. Menoux. I should excuse myself for
receiving you like this. But you know how my corns make
me suffer in the evening. All of my fatigue goes to my
feet."

The young teacher closed the door. It bore the number
twenty-two. He was not mistaken. Michelet must have
changed rooms during his absence, unless Mrs. Blanet had
decided to throw him out. He descended the stairs, humming, and stuck his head into the salon.

"Good evening, Mrs. Blanet. I hope that you are feeling well. Still doing the wash?"

"Ah, it's not funny to wash the sheets of twenty dirty tenants with this damn powdered soap. They call this soap? I call it rubbish!"

"You're quite right, but—"

"No buts about it! And all of the tenants take advantage by dirtying more than ever. I think they collect filth all day long just to wipe themselves in the evening on my sheets. There is even one who blows his nose in them. I will end up taking away all of your sheets. You could always buy a charcoal sack to sleep in."

"I realize that it isn't funny," agreed St. Menoux. "But tell me, what have you done with Mr. Michelet?"

"Mr. Michelet? What Mr. Michelet?"

"Good heavens! There is only one in your hotel. The architect—the old fool."

"The fool? I thought that was you," said Mrs. Blanet, shrugging her shoulders. "I suspected this would happen to you one day with all your numbers. There has never been a Mr. Michelet in my hotel. Miss Brigitte has been living in Room Twenty-two for the past six years. You know that as well as I. You have been her neighbor for a long time. By the way, she has to get rid of her cat. He pisses everywhere, and it's infectious. And when there isn't enough around to feed people, I ask you—is this the time to have animals?"

"St. Menoux climbed up to his room in a dream. On opening the door of Room Twenty-two he had seen a strange decor and had been astonished to hear himself addressed as "Mr. St. Menoux" by a stranger. He should have recognized her. It was Brigitte, the old seamstress. He now only remembered her. He had always seen her at Number Twenty-two, that was true.

But Mr. Michelet?

Which Mr. Michelet?

He took his forehead in his hands and tried to hold on

to the fleeing images. He saw himself on the sidewalk, sharing his bread card. He pulled out his wallet. His bread card was complete, hardly used. When he held it in his hands he no longer remembered why he had felt the need to examine it. He shook his head two or three times. "Michelet! Michelet! The name did not remind him of anything more than an ordinary school problem.

"My last adventure definitely shook my mind," he murmured.

He sat at his table, pushed aside the papers and books which covered it and began his homework, examining the pictures from the Canon Chamayou's book which he had taken from the noelite safe.

He found two new chapters in it. The first related the "attack" on the jeweler; the courageous conduct of the brave islander; the "dramatic chase in the streets of Paris"; the arrest of the bandit, "his escape under mysterious circumstances"; the scandal, the investigation committee; the charge against the guard, the ward and chief of police; the examining magistrate and his suicide; the resignation of the Ministers of Justice, and the Ministerial crisis.

The other chapter, which was shorter, related the appearance of the Green Devil at the town hall of the Eleventh District and stated that Miss Martin-Marin, the fiancée, had been so frightened that she fell gravely ill. The marriage was not celebrated that day or later, because the unfortunate girl, who seemed to have gone mad, fell into a fainting spell each time she saw her future husband. She identified him with the Green Devil and confused the acceptance of marriage with the acceptance of the devil.

The canon added a few pious commentaries and two phrases of compassion for the young girl and her fiancé, Mr. Michelet.

Michelet!

In a flash, memories sprang into St. Menoux's mind. He again saw the little bearded architect.

He rose quickly, upsetting his chair. He had just figured it out.

"Certainly! He no longer exists. He never existed, since his parents did not marry!"

He sat down again, trembling in excitement before this extraordinary event. He hastily drew on a white sheet of paper an approximate portrait of the vanished man and noted all that he remembered about him.

He referred to the canon's account from time to time to find a new starting point. However, he finally had to stop. He no longer knew if he was remembering or inventing.

He had written "chalet." It was the most vivid image that remained in his memory. He recalled perfectly the over-elaborate house. It must have disappeared along with its author. He wondered what other building had grown in its place. He rose, went to the window and saw with astonishment that the strange ramshackle house was still there. Against the dark blue sky, dotted with stars, he saw the black silhouette of its bellturrets and odd roof. It was illogical. He decided to examine it closer the next day.

He spent a restless night, waking up several times, feeling of his familiar objects—his alarm clock and his slippers—to assure him that he had returned to his normal time period.

When he opened his window, his eyes, still blurred with sleep, were filled with the image of the mosaic cat and all the grotesque menagerie which climbed, on the other side of the road, the chimneys of Michelet's house. He dressed hurriedly, crossed the boulevard and read with great astonishment on the stone, tinted rose by a beautiful morning sun, these engraved words: "Alexander Jaretier, architect."

The same building had found another architect to build it! The young professor, his head lowered, his hands clasped behind his back, walked slowly toward the subway. He stopped to reflect, then walked on again, talking to himself.

Was it therefore necessary for the world's progress that this horrible piece of masonry exist in this exact spot? Our small solar system is invisible in the infinite. Paris on the earth? An imperceptible wart. What importance is there for the universe if Paris has one house more or less?

However, the man who was supposed to build it precisely between these piles of charcoal and this furniture warehouse and to decorate it in such a ludicrous manner was not born. Another one appeared who accomplished exactly the same task.

Therefore, if Louis XIII did not have a child, his successor would still have been the Sun King? And even if Eiffel died at an early age of an attack of croup or scarlet fever, Paris would still possess its famous tower?

St. Menoux realized that events modified by his own interventions in the last century were purely human and that he had changed nothing in the face of the world nor in the evolution of history.

He felt humiliated in his human pride. Were he and his human brothers really only bits of charcoal in the eternal furnace? Their lives were burning. Each soul, each heart added to the common flame. And the turbine turned as it must turn.

Each individual's destiny was perhaps susceptible to modifications, but the destiny of mankind remained inexorable. The mass of men could not avoid the catastrophes which were awaiting them at the turn of the centuries.

Thus Essaillon's plan to work for happiness had proven absolutely in vain. By the strength of goodness, patience and love, it was undoubtedly possible to extricate a man or a woman from the quicksand of ennui and suffering in which we all flounder. Yet nothing and no one can prevent the multitude from rushing toward its doom. And noelite is a useless invention unless it plays a role in the removal of the future evils of humanity. Why must humanity experience so many wars and revolutions and bathe in an ocean of hate, pain and blood?

These were the questions that rushed through St. Menoux's mind while the subway carried him toward the Racine villa. The name God resounded in him like a bell.

3

"Let's get married," proposed Annette. "Why wait any longer? I was so afraid I had lost you. . ." She was standing, her golden hands clinging to the sleeves of Peter's vest, at the height of his biceps. She lifted her head toward him and he marveled at the purity of her eyes.

Men raise only their eyelids when they look at each other, while hard glass doors remain closed between them. But some unselfish beings, when they look at those they love, open this door to their eyes. Their look is then a road without deceit to their warm soul. Annette looked at Peter with her naked eyes, and he was overcome. He did not understand how he was able to inspire such a love. He was almost frightened by the gift so simple and so complete that he read in the clear liquid of these eyes. He was not sure if he was strong enough or stable enough to deserve such confidence. He loved Annette, but his feeling seemed measured by her feelings toward him. Perhaps he would have preferred a more restrained love.

Then he gave in completely to those open eyes, reveled in their flame, swelled his thin chest and for a few seconds joined his heart with hers. But that lasted only a moment. He became himself again. He felt ashamed because he was not as honest in his feelings as in his reason. His state of mind did not correspond to the young girl's, and seemed as false to him as an equation whose two terms on each side of the equal sign do not balance. She could not imagine that different intensities and qualities of love could exist. She loved

Peter and Peter loved her. That seemed very simple to her.

She asked him to move into the villa again. She did not care
about social conventions. Peter was more bourgeois. But he
stifled his scruples and took the bedroom which he had
occupied during Essaillon's lifetime. He moved without any
help; he feared too much for his treasures. He felt the
greatest pain in loading his three trunks into the cart with
the assistance of a street vendor. He piled his books helter-
skelter on the floor of the light covered cart, threw a few
clothes on top of it all, pushed, moaned and cast off. Mrs.
Blanet waved good-bye with her broom and wiped her eyes
with her sleeve. He gave her as a souvenir some earrings
with tear-shaped pearls and a lapis lazuli hat pin.

The cart shaft shook and jumped out of St. Menoux's
thin hands. He almost capsized twenty times and was almost
crushed by the only bus which still ran in Paris. The enormous
engine with its gas tank on the back stopped a foot short
of him with screeching brakes.

"There's a big shot for you," shouted the conductor.

Peter, so thin, did not have the courage to smile at hearing
himself thus qualified. He wiped his forehead, started again
and finally arrived dead tired.

He did not seem entirely happy since moving nearer to
Annette. The girl sometimes found him seated at a table,
his head in his hands, his face crushed by some haunting
thought. When she spoke to him, he often did not answer.
She would raise her head and see him, with his tormented
forehead, dreaming with lost eyes. When she softly waved
her hand in his field of vision, he would come back to earth,
blush and excuse himself.

After two weeks he had grown even thinner and more
hunched over. His skin stretched across his bony nose.

Annette, upset, wanted to know the reason for his worry.

He answered, smiling, that it was nothing and continued to languish in his reverie in the house and garden.

Twice she surprised him in the laboratory rummaging through the iron cupboards. But she kept the key to the closet where the diving suits were locked. She did not want to see her happiness escape her again.

She set the marriage date and hurried through the formalities. Peter seemed to be happy again. Annette blushed each morning at the thought that one day less separated her from the time when she would be his wife. She took her time dressing. She wanted to soften further the texture of her skin. She looked at herself and found herself beautiful. She caressed her breasts and hips and burst out laughing, happy for him over the gift which she was going to give him, sent kisses to him through the walls and splashed bath water everywhere.

As the marriage day approached, Peter became more somber. He had thought that the happiness of finally possessing Annette would chase away his insane ideas. Yet they remained, rulers of his mind. For several weeks a world of such strange thoughts filled his mind, and he planned out such an extraordinary project, that the joys of his heart and senses seemed futile and without importance by comparison.

One week before the set date, he could no longer stand it. He decided to speak to Annette.

It was in the evening in the garden. An early spring had followed the mild winter. The sky was pink between the transparent leaves. Annette was sitting in the large wicker chair and Peter was on the grass at her feet. In the distance the noises of the town were heard, the roaring of an isolated truck and the procession of a coach's iron wheels along the pavement. In the branches a sleeping bird sometimes fluttered about. Another uttered a small cry of contentment and well-being.

Peter placed his head on Annette's knees and she ran her fingers over his hair.

"Peter, my Peter," she said sweetly. "I'm so happy." He did not move. He did not answer immediately. He was happy too. What madness was going to lead him away from this peace? It was almost in spite of himself that he spoke.

"Annie. Annette," he said in a very low voice, soft as twilight. "You know how much I love you. You are my entire life. For me you are the flowers of the world, all light, the blue of the heavens, song, the fresh growing grass and the morning dew. My love, the day that approaches, which will give you to me, completely abandoned in my arms, burns me with the joy of the sun. When I think of the sweet moment when you will belong to me, my heart pounds and my blood is like fired gold. I would like to hurry through this marvelous hour which will remove all that still separates us and that will make us a single being forever more. And yet—

Annette, her head thrown back over the back of the chair, her eyes closed, felt her body melt and her senses lulled by the sweetness of his words of love.

Her hair, spread out on the wicker chair, began to mingle with the night. The last words woke her like a cold shower. She sat up erect. "And yet?" she asked apprehensively.

St. Menoux summoned all his courage. "And yet, my darling. I feel that I shall never be completely happy if I leave unanswered in my mind a certain question that tortures me. You know your father and I had a mission. Your father could not continue. His overweight condition, his asthma, his weak heart, the poisoning of his blood were undoubtedly the essential factors in his discouragement. For my part, I wish to continue and to still try, after a period of rest and reflection, to find within the course of the centuries the causes of man's great agony."

He got up. Annette scarcely saw him in the deepening night. His head was lost in the leaves of the lowest branches. He began again in a hollow voice, "You have helped me with your love and your science. But one of my recent observations tragically poses the question of man's destiny.

If the conclusions suggested to me by this question are correct, then it is necessary to renounce all action and to huddle in the hand of God, while appealing to his mercy."

Annette shivered. The evening's dampness penetrated her clothes and placed its cold hands on her skin. She pulled her long hair over her neck and bosom. Her heart was as black as the night. She knew that Peter was going to leave again.

"I must," said the voice falling from the leaves. "I must verify this observation. I must try a last experiment. If it produces the results that I expect, then I will come back to you forever. I shall burn the diving suit and I shall no longer think of the happiness of others, but of yours alone, my love."

Annette rose in turn and leaned against Peter's chest. She heard the heavy beating of his heart and the hollow rumble of his voice.

"You must give me the key to the iron cupboard. You must help me prepare for my next and last expedition. I cannot escape the obligations of my thoughts. Help me fulfill my duty and the marvelous day that approaches will be a reward for us—a climax and a happiness as pure as a diamond."

Annette sighed. "Peter, I will help you."

The next day they began their work. To avoid an accident like the one that had almost separated him from Annette, St. Menoux wanted to wear three diving suits, one on top of the other. The two women stayed up for four days and nights to cut them out and sew them. Peter soaked all his underwear in the noelite—undershirt, pants, socks. He did not want to tell his fiancée the goal of his mission. He feared that she would argue and ask him to put off his voyage. All was ready for Friday evening.

When the moment came for his departure, Annette helped her fiancé to harness himself. She bit her lips so as not to burst into tears.

Peter took her distressed face in his hands. "My darling," he said sweetly. You must not be sorrowful nor fearful. I will return before ten o'clock tomorrow morning. There is no danger. You know I have taken all precautions."

Annette nodded. She did not dare open her mouth for fear that her pain would cry out. She was sadder than she was worried. Sad to see that on the eve of this great day, he could think of something other than her. Sad to read in his eyes such an exultation caused by something other than her love. Sad that he kept a secret from her.

He verified the contents of his knapsacks, held out a piece of paper to the girl and disappeared while kissing her on the lips.

She wanted to read his message but when she lowered her eyes, her tears overflowed. She made a great effort, blew her nose, wiped her eyes and read these words: I am leaving for Toulon, July 12, 1793, exactly three o'clock in the morning.

"Gee-up! Dirty beast! She-ass! Gee-up! You old jackass, gee-up!"

The shafts groaned, the traces grated and the horseshoes sounded on the cobblestone road. The heavy wheels danced around their axles. Against the summer night sky, the file of carriages stood out as in a shadow theater. St. Menoux, asleep in the ditch, breathed with emotion the smell of the military convoy—odors of leather, of dung, of the sweat of men and horses mingled together.

For a moment he believed he had returned to 1940. He recognized the silhouettes of the same wagons, of the same carriages with which he had entered Belgium on May 10. He thought he heard Credent's voice swearing by the thunder.

He remembered with melancholy the painful months lived among his comrades, the wonderful brotherhood which united men of all classes and the nonhypocritical egoism which put them in opposition when necessary. Sighing, he pushed on the vibrator. This was not the time to dream.

He crossed through the convoy. A heavy wagon loaded with kegs had turned over by the side of the road. One horizontal wheel turned slowly in the air. The fallen horse, crushed by the shaft, tried to get up, struggling in the night. A barrel had broken the legs of a howling soldier. A cluster of men unloaded the wagon, hurrying around the beast in the light of a lantern.

"Cut his traces here. Good God! Get out of there, imbecile, before he gives you a swift kick!"

The yellow lantern light illuminated strange uniforms and the sunburnt face of a hard-boiled old man with a moustache, wearing a hat with two points, who was commanding the maneuvers. A flask of wine was shining on the ground.

St. Menoux passed by, crossed the vehicles and beasts who were pulling strenuously, and arrived at the head of the convoy, where a troop of infantry men were marching to the rhythm of a song, *The Canteen-keeper's Apricot.*

The voyager overheard from conversations that the convoy was carrying munitions and provisions to the advance camp of attackers, a village conquered the night before, at the top of a hill which dominated the countryside.

St. Menoux went ahead of the convoy. Morning came and the young teacher began to look around him. Some soldiers were sleeping outdoors in ditches, on straw or dry grass. Others were perched in the olive trees. From a bulging cask, wedged by large stones, there projected two feet wrapped in rags and a snore. Around a fire some elongated shadows rose and fell in their sleep.

St. Menoux reached the village. At dawn the first houses stood against the sky, their black walls still smoking. A sentinel, a grenadier with gray sidewhiskers, gaitered down to his thighs and rifle over his shoulder, walked back and forth across the road.

In a corner of the great square the cooks were hanging a copper cauldron on the shaft of a cart, and lighting a fire under it. The youngest, a swarthy-looking person on all fours, was blowing on the crackling twigs. He had his hair braided like an old soldier and his straight tress of hair danced on his neck.

"Whoof! Whoof!" a large dirty fellow, dressed in a round red vest and black breeches cut at the knees shouted encouragingly. "You will never blow as hard as the inhabitants of Saint Bandolfe blew at the horse's ass."

He threw some vegetables, herbs and potatoes into the cauldron. He wore a tasseled hat so dirty that its original color could not be ascertained. He coughed and spit out a big glob to clear his throat.

Around the village the crickets were silent. A pair of blackbirds niched in a plane tree welcomed dawn with a shower of whistles. A horse neighed, waking the entire stable. A bat crossed the square in zigzag, hurrying toward his home in the ruins of an old castle. A wood pigeon, swollen with love, warbled a song from his round throat. Each minute new voices were added to the birds' concert. A company fire crackled close by.

"Tsh!" said the big cook, wiping his nose with the back of his fist, "it's these bastards that they're shooting!"

"Which bastards?" asked his aide, who spoke in a shrill voice.

"Good grief, I don't know. Some villagers that they arrested yesterday after the battle. We must set an example."

"Woman! Where did you hide the bacon?"

A woman's nervous laugh was heard. It rose and then suddenly became silent.

"Some don't waste any time! The lard? It's in the barrel behind you. No, not that one. That's the cod. You can't even find the end of your nose in the middle of your face!"

From all of the doors, soldiers now came out, stretching their limbs, yawning and prowling around the cooks' fire. They were all ages, young ones and old ones. Some were wearing the uniform, a blue outfit with white vest and white breeches. But most of them did not even possess any part of a uniform. Instead, they substituted civilian clothes, dirty, torn, patched up with different pieces. They wore shapeless caps of knotted rags and had tattered shoes, or none at all. Barefoot tramps and ragged men seemed as joyous as those who wore a new uniform or beautiful English boots taken from the enemy.

One volunteer whose white breeches were torn all over stretched out a large green curtain on the ground, took off his trousers, laid them on the woolen goods and began to cut out a new pair of breeches with his cutlass.

The convoy announced itself in the distance by the song of "Mrs. Veto," sung by the detachment which preceded it at the top of its voice. It was a company on horseback clothed in green and wearing a small vest and a cardboard helmet.

A few gunshots were heard nearby. A drum in the village beat to arms. In the country, others answered it. In a flash, disorder ceased. The soldiers grouped around their officers. Some noncommissioned officers bawled out. Red and blue dragoons on work horses galloped across the village. Some infantry detachments followed, rifles in hand.

"It's the besieged army making a sally," said the large cook. "Jules saw them from the edge of the village. There are red ones and yellow ones. Spaniards and English. Drink your soup."

St. Menoux, invisible, followed the soldiers who hurried toward the battle. At the village exit, the hill began to descend toward a valley where a little river glimmered. On the other side a rocky slope climbed toward a stronghold, whose freshly dug earth made an ochre spot against the gray countryside. The sea stretched out to the right, shining in the sun's early rays. Peter noticed, a few miles away, a fleet anchored in the port of Toulon.

The besieged townspeople had already cleared the river and were visible at the bottom of the hill as the soldiers of the National Convention joined them shouting, "Long live the Republic!" A furious conflict began, whirling and plunging in the two-foot-deep water of the stream, and climbed the other slope. The red, the yellow, the blue, the green and the white of the uniforms mingled, regrouped, dispersed again, crumbled and congealed under the light veil of powder smoke that the morning wind rolled and carried to the sea.

The advantage seemed to turn quickly to the French. The red uniforms climbed again toward the stronghold. The yellow followed. The dragoons pushed ahead behind heavy sabre blows. But the cavaliers halted before the fusillade from the fortress.

St. Menoux, overwhelmed by the sight, forgot the goal of his voyage. He suddenly jumped so violently that he was projected toward the sky and beyond the highest plane tree. A thunderous roar had just burst behind him; the artillery was strafing the fugitives. He flew among the frightened birds and the projectiles, which roared in his ears. The noise of the cannons was more muffled and less brutal than the noise of modern cannons. There were eight installed on the top of a hill at the gate of the village.

Peter crossed a cloud of black smoke, slowly descending toward the battle. There he should find the man he was looking for.

The artillerymen moved purposefully, stuffing the load of powder, rolling the cannon balls into the mouths of the cannon, pointing them and readying the fuses.

A small man with a dry voice commanded them. St. Menoux recognized him. The artillery lieutenant wore a blue uniform with black trim and white pants, rather wide, buttoned on both sides from the hip to the ankle. A shiny three-cornered hat rested on his thin head. The middle corner was placed over his right ear and from the other two, black ribbons floated in the wind.

The traveler approached and stared at the man with a passionate curiosity. The glorious morning sun framed his profile in gold. He shouted out brief orders, from time to time scratching his fists, his groin, his armpits, then crossing his hands again behind his back. His flat hair fell down his neck, hiding his ears. St. Menoux found him very small and rather yellowish.

He certainly lacks grandeur, he thought.

He sighed heavily and prepared for action. He had come to kill Bonaparte.

Napoleon had crushed Europe under his heel. Modern nations still carry the scars of his footsteps. He was not led by men, but imposed his will upon them. The entire adventure was a result of his personal genius. Had he died at the beginning of his career, had a stray bullet killed him during the seige of Toulon, what would this have done to history?

St. Menoux had asked himself this question for weeks. He would have to resolve it before committing himself completely to Annette. If Bonaparte were killed and another emperor were to rise from the army or from the people and wage the same wars, it would be proof that men are not really free, but that a terrible fate leads them along a bloody road traced for all eternity, with no hope of changing its direction. The wise man, then, will reject the active life, will leave the ignorant to their quarrels, and will savor the simple daily joys of a secluded place.

Peter smiled tenderly at Annette's image. He would build a paradise with his young wife, in a chosen corner of space and time, in an epoch sheltered from storms and revolutions. They would live there for years, for centuries, for eternity. They would only love each other. Nothing else to do? Well, he would see.

Now he would undertake his final experiment. This evening he would discover the destiny of man. This evening he would be Annette's husband. Little Annette! Sweet of body and in heart. This evening . . .

The combatant's cries, the roar of explosions, the red light of the rising sun on the clouds and the sea, and the consciousness of the enormity of his task excited St. Menoux. With arms stretched out, he soared and circled the small man encamped in the smoky haze. His thin hands touched the face and the back of the future ruler of Europe. He looked for the best place to strike.

The black ribbons of the three-cornered hat and Bonaparte's black hair floated in the morning wind. His clear eyes watched the cannon balls ravage row upon row of the distant enemy. Undoubtedly he was already dreaming of taking the city. Victory, conquest, power—the invisible finger of death was touching his shoulder.

In order to act, St. Menoux would have to stop for a few seconds outside of time. It would be brief. He decided to station himself behind the man, to appear, shoot, and disappear.

A violent explosion shook the ground. A cloud of dust flooded the battery. Shots whistled and roared. Pebbles crackled in the plane tree leaves. A severed arm flew by St. Menoux. The cannon of the fortress replied and the dust flew. A bomb-burst mangled two gunners. Bonaparte did not move, but continued to shout out orders. The hesitant artillerymen went back to their posts, directing their fire on the fort.

Peter did not want to take any chances. He would shoot from behind a shelter. A bundle of sticks four feet from his victim would do the trick. He stepped behind them like a puff of smoke and stretched out, glued to the ground. It was perfect. Now he was ready to alter the destiny of the world. He was overcome with emotion. He tried to breathe slowly and waited for his heartbeat to quiet and for his hands to stop trembling. He reasoned with himself. This was as simple as a geometry problem. He regained his composure. Let's go.

He stopped the vibrator. The odor of powder stung his nose. Cannons pounded the air and a bomb approached with a deafening roar. It exploded. He fired. An artilleryman had thrown himself between the bomb and Bonaparte. It did not explode. The man was struck by four bullets. Two others whistled in his ears. He staggered. Bonaparte did not move. Eight cannons roared and the ground trembled. St. Menoux had no more bullets in his weapon. The smoke was choking him. The weight of destiny was crushing him. He had failed. He became invisible again.

Why hadn't he brought another ammunition clip? He had
not known that a clenched finger fires an automatic pistol
like a machine gun. Hē had never used a firearm, not even
during the war. He was neither a warrior nor an assassin, only
a scientist, a theorist. He would have to begin all over
again. He slumped discouraged and terribly weary. He did
not move from his spot. The artillery continued to thunder.
He floated behind the blind like a cork on still water. His
enthusiasm left him as the cannon balls burst from the brown
steel cannons. A heavy sadness replaced his excitement, perhaps fatigue.

The soldier's devotion did not surprise him. He knew that
he had been rescued before by the fanatic love of his men
at the Arcole bridge and at the siege of Acre. Yet here, it
seemed that God himself had pushed the gunner in front of
the weapon that would have altered the course of history.
God did not want the face of the world to be changed.

Bonaparte pointed to the man fallen at his feet. Two
gunners, wounded by the cannonfire, lifted him slowly and
carried him to shelter. The little lieutenant scratched his
left wrist. The firing continued.

St. Menoux stretched out his arms, slid along the ground,
and approached the wounded man laid out in the shelter of
a plane tree trunk. How tall and thin he was! Peter bent his
invisible face over this pale face.

His eyes were closed, his fine nose stiff. Traces of black
spotted his cheeks and his forehead. His blond hair, straight
from sweat and dust, hung in the grass. A soft, pale gold
moustache spanned his upper lip. The man must have been
about eighteen years old. At twenty he probably would not
have been capable of such an act of love. He moved an arm
and groaned without opening his eyes. His comrades tore open
his uniform and bandaged his shoulder and thigh with shirt
rags.

"They are little splinters," said one to the other. "Perhaps
he will pull through."

Screaming death spewed from the cannons. Above the hill

rolled clouds of smoke. The wounded man and the two hobbled gunners huddled together. They were all the same age and had the same blond hair. Perhaps they came from the same village. The smallest of the three, one with the reddest face, rubbed his peasant hands together. He looked at his outstretched comrade.

"Poor Durdat. He would have been discharged soon!"

The words from his mouth added their tiny vibrations to the storm of noise, and drifted away in clouds of smoke.

"Durdat!" remarked Peter. "That was my mother's name."

The two men returned to combat. The little thickset boy walked right through the voyager. St. Menoux, touched, stood up and sat in the tree trunk, his head bent over the head of the wounded boy, tall and thin and blond like himself. If this hair were cut and the shadow of a mustache cut, he would resemble him like a brother.

Remorse gripped St. Menoux. He wanted to help the poor fellow, bandage his wounds, ask his forgiveness and kiss the face so similar to his own.

He was suddenly seized by a horrible thought. He had just remembered what his mother had told him when he was studying the wars of the Revolution and of the Empire.

"Your grandfather's grandfather," she had said to him, "emerged from all of these wars without a scratch. He began as a simple gunner. At Waterloo he was a captain. He was over forty when he finally married."

"The Emperor spoke of him in his memoirs," she added proudly. "He called him 'my faithful Joachim'. There were two brothers. One was killed in Russia."

The cannons were silent. The wind carried the smoke in long wisps. Beyond, the red fort emerged from a gray cloud. The wounded and the dead dotted the valley with vivid colors. A riderless horse galloped, stopped short, kicked, neighed, approached the river at a trot and took a long drink. A hesitant cricket sawed the air with a testing cry, then repeated and accelerated his song. The wounded groaned and one of them, close by, cursed without stopping in a low rumbling voice.

St. Menoux's whole body trembled. His teeth were chattering. This man that he had just struck down was obviously one of the Durdat brothers. He was, perhaps, Peter's own ancestor.

Now a thousand crickets were crying with joy on the sunny banks.

"The sea smells good," said a passing soldier.

St. Menoux kneeled near the wounded man. How would he know? A shadow cut the outstretched body in two. The voyager raised his head. Bonaparte was standing over him. He looked down at the boy who had saved his life. Without saying a word, impassive, he made a sign to carry him away. They laid him on a stretcher. A drop of blood fell through St. Menoux, capturing a blade of grass.

Catherine set the wedding table—two place settings on a lace tablecloth. Crystal glasses which sang when touched slightly, a garland of white lilacs, a small table, two golden straw chairs, and then the door of the pink and white bedroom.

The young maid closed the shutters and lit the lamps. She thought that soon she might marry too. Her beau was waiting for her in Normandy. Before leaving they had agreed to it. It had been a tepid night under an apple tree. She had felt the tree trunk climb to the sky and all the stars flowing in her body. She tightened her arms around her bosom and blushed. Shrugging her shoulders, she ran to her oven.

Peter and Annette were married in the Thirteenth District. The priest blessed them in the intimacy of the sacristy. At the town hall, they took their witnesses from the shoe line. St. Menoux thanked them with packets of cigarettes. Before returning, Annette wanted to see his bachelor bedroom.

Mrs. Blanet received them emotionally. "Ah, Mr. St. Menoux, you have found a very pretty wife. Very nice. Congratulations. If my poor Gaston were only here—" She wiped her eyes.

They drank the *aperitif* that she served them, sniffling—some authentic port from Potin's. The last bottle.

All three climbed the stairs.

"Excuse me, but I'll go ahead," said Mrs. Blanet. "I will open the door for you. Mr. Garnier is usually not at home at this hour. He works at Billancourt. He is the new tenant in your room. Please excuse the disorder. It's not that he is dirty, but I didn't gain much in the exchange when you left. Come in. What an old pig, just the same. Mrs. St. Menoux, I beg your pardon. They make me talk rubbish. They are all alike. They leave everything all around."

Neither Peter nor Annette were listening to her. Annette looked tenderly at the narrow gray room, the iron bed, the table of white wood, the unmade bed and the colorless curtains. She slowly withdrew her arm from her husband's. Crossing the room with quiet steps, she opened the window and looked out at the world he had seen each day.

He joined her and placed his hands on her soft shoulders. He saw only her.

"What a strange house," she said in a low voice.

He raised his eyes. In the dimming evening sky, the grotesque silhouette of Mr. Michelet's pavilion—it's odd roof, the strange bell turrets and the sneering beasts—rose ominously.

"Kitty! Kitty! Come my little kitten," called Miss Brigitte from the neighboring room.

St. Menoux suddenly drew Annette against him, lifted her, carried her out of the room and fled, descending the stairs in a rush. Did Mrs. Blanet protest? It was Mr. Michelet, the dirty phantom of the architect who pursued him and jumped down the stairs behind him.

They broke out onto the boulevard; the passers-by, the clear sky and the waiting bicycle-taxi.

The two men in sweaters pumped the pedals curving their backs like drawn bows. Annette, snuggled against Peter, did not open her eyes. He did not open his arms closed around her.

He had followed the stretcher carrying the wounded boy to a large room in the old castle. There were about a hundred stretched out on the straw, crying and shouting. The heat rose, adding to their fever. One man, clothed in vivid colors, wearing a large hat topped with feathers, entered and said a few words of encouragement to the first wounded. He left quickly, repulsed by the odor of corrupted blood, dirty sweaty feet and excrement from the dying bodies. He took three steps outdoors and vomited in the grass.

The passing surgeon waved him a jeering hello. He was a large red strapping fellow, clothed in breeches of black material turning slightly green and a white shirt with rolled-up sleeves. He carried his instruments in a sack of black serge. He entered the castle deliberately. He examined the wounded one after another, designating those he would attend to immediately. Arriving in front of Durdat, he said, "Two little splinters in the thigh, one in the arm. He will pull through. I'll take care of him this evening. There are some more urgent cases."

Peter bent over him in the thick air and listened apprehensively. The words reassured him. He waited longer, prowled around and tried in vain to learn Durdat's first name. Durdat, his lips tight, was gasping in little breaths. He had not regained consciousness.

Peter had to leave. He had told Annette, "I will return at ten o'clock tomorrow morning." He went back. The young girl was waiting for him. When he appeared she opened her clasped hands and her eyes filled with tears of joy. It seemed to St. Menoux that he had just waked up from a nightmare. He felt so lively, so solid! He felt his body, placed his hands on the cold marble and caressed his fiancée's hair. He left the diving suits stacked in a pile, bathed and ate.

He was near the one he loved. What was there to fear? All that was an absurd dream. Even if the man he had wounded was his ancestor, hadn't the surgeon assured that he would recover? And then, he was probably only his grandfather's grandfather's brother.

St. Menoux relaxed. He looked at Annette and smiled at her. He was there, very much alive, near his loved one. Of his fears, only remorse remained. He promised himself to return tomorrow to the convoy at exactly the same moment. He would travel the same road, cross the camp, reach the village, find the thundering battery and the little lieutenant with the black ribbons and the tall gunner with the moustache. Then, instead of shooting, he would throw his loaded revolver into the brush. The gunner would not be wounded and Bonaparte would follow his destiny. So much for history. So much for science. Why this absurd need to know? If men wish to be happy, let them find their own happiness!

He would hold his love close to him in the taxi, skipping along the cobbled streets to the Racine Villa. Mr. Michelet's ghost would no longer mock him. Peter's destiny had nothing in common with the old man's. Even when he was alive, Michelet was no more than a ghost. He had only to disappear to no longer exist. Why not be happy and forget about what had happened? The marriage began and the day came to an end.

The day ended. Two men carried the naked wounded soldier to a table covered with a bloody sheet. The weary surgeon was astonished to see that the man was so pale. Two pieces of shrapnel in his thigh and one in his shoulder? His eyes were closed and his stomach extremely hard. He examined him more closely and furrowed his brow. He made a sign to take him back and wiped his forehead with a hairy forearm. That was it. Certainly. Near the kidney there was a small violet hole. He stood erect and made a sweeping gesture. "Don't bother, he's finished. There's a piece of shrapnel in his gut. He won't last the night. Next."

Night came. The wounded man was close to death. His

hands clawed at the straw. The wounded, young and old, were groaning or crying. It was warm in the large gloomy room. It was warm in the pink and white bedroom of the villa.

Peter opened the door. His heart beat so fast that it almost hurt. Was it only emotion? Annette was waiting for him in the large warm bed. Annette—her soft body, his beloved, his wife.

She waited for him. The wind that ushered in the night whispered in the trees around the house. A motor roared at the horizon. The door opened. There he was.

She turned out all the lights. Peter, her Peter, was here! How cold he was. His body was icy! She opened her arms to him and opened herself entirely for him. Her heart flew— flew into joy, into the sun. Peter, her husband! God, how light he was in bed, how light on her! Like smoke, like a shadow! She scarcely felt him. It seemed that she was dreaming.

A sergeant entered the large black room, holding an oil lamp in his hand. A sphere of yellow light circled its wick. He moved it above the wounded. A soldier who was checking a list accompanied him. From time to time they stopped before a silent body. They neared the blond gunner. His fingers were unclenched; his eyes were finally open. He stared into the darkness.

The man with the list bent over, made a sign to the sergeant to lower his lamp, read a name written in charcoal on the wall, looked for it on his paper, moistened his pencil with his tongue and marked a cross next to *Durdat, Joachim*.

One A.M. sounded in the Tremplin-le-Haut belfry. In her white virginal bed, Annette awoke suddenly. Who had called her?

Someone needed help. In the street someone was shouting. Someone let out a horrible cry. A voice she recognized called her by name in indescribable despair. And then the voice was lost in the night, in death. She jumped out of bed and trembling, lit a lamp. She recognized the voice, but the name that filled her heart would not come to her lips. She no longer knew it, and yet, she knew it. She took the lamp in her hand and left the bedroom. Her long nightgown brushed the red vestibule tile. Her long black hair fell across her shoulders. She passed before a door outlined with light. Her father was still working in his bed. Once more he would continue his impossible research until dawn. Nothing, neither war nor invasion, nor the anxieties of the armistice, could distract him from his fruitless work. Poor dear stubborn father.

She reached the front door. She was now wide awake. The anguish of deep sleep had left her. She raised the lamp above her head and opened the door. The lamp drew a square of light on the street. Very high in the stars a motor was humming. The moon illuminated the empty street. A tiny whirlwind climbed the three steps and laid a dead leaf at her naked feet.

Paris, 1942-1943

The End

Postscript

Postscript

TO BE
AND NOT TO BE

You read the words "The End" a few seconds ago. I wrote them fifteen years ago, and yet—

Yet for St. Menoux there could be no end.

Think for a moment. He killed his ancestor before he had time to marry and have children. So he disappeared, that's understood. He doesn't exist and he never did exist. There never was a Peter St. Menoux.

Good.

Yet if St. Menoux does not exist, and he never did exist, *he could not have killed his ancestor!*

Therefore his ancestor continued his destiny normally, married, and had children, who had children, who had children.

And one day Peter St. Menoux was born, lived, grew up, met Essaillon, explored the year 100,000, wished to kill Bonaparte, and killed his ancestor.

So far, so good.

He killed his ancestor.

Therefore he does not exist.

Therefore he did not kill his ancestor.

Therefore he exists.

Therefore he killed his ancestor.

Therefore he does not exist.

Stop, this is madness. Think!

No, it is not a vortex of life and death, an instantaneous and fixed succession of two contrary destinies. St. Menoux does not alternately exist and not exist. Both states exist at the same time. His two destinies (or rather his destiny and his nondestiny) are simultaneous. From the moment his ancestor died, St. Menoux both does and does not exist, because not existing he could not kill and from this fact, he exists and kills.

"To be or not to be?" asks Hamlet. To be *and* not to be, replies St. Menoux.

It is not without bewilderment and remorse that I consider the terrifying adventure into which I sent this tall, pale boy. He lived in me for many months, more intimately than a fetus within its mother. I brought him into a painful world and thousands of people saw him live and act. And you? You know him well. You know his feelings, his ambitions, his shyness, and his remorse. You could almost draw his portrait with your eyes closed. He is your friend. He is my child. And so he left us to go . . . To go where? Not to go where? To become and not to become what?

I do not know what to say to you. It is impossible for me to imagine such a state. For our human minds, limited and feeble, only the "or" of Hamlet is comprehensible. The "or" already carries enough anguish. The "and" of St. Menoux destroys our equilibrium. We are at the outer limit of our rational universe. One step more, one word more, and it is the beginning of the abyss, the logic of the absurd and the confirmation of the possibility of the impossible.

That is where St. Menoux is—and where he is not. At the same time living and nonliving, black and white on the same face, heavy and light with the same weight, departed before having arrived.

No metaphor can help us. The nature of his existence is beyond us. The only ones who might have a vague idea of it are the great physicists of our time, specialists in the constituent particles of the atom. Because all they know about these particles, all that irrefutable mathematical logic has taught them about these particles is that at each moment they are neither somewhere nor elsewhere, neither here nor there, neither nowhere nor everywhere.

And yet it is these improbable particles revolving around nothingness that constitute the paper of this book, your hand, your eye that reads it and your worrying brain. Disquieting, terrifying, vagabond particles of your body—they are never in their place and yet never elsewhere. There is nothing between them and where they are, there is nothing.

Then you. What are you?

To be and not to be, that is the question. Unless it is the answer.

R.B.
March 1958

OTHER AWARD BOOKS
YOU'LL BE SURE TO ENJOY

The jolting, tumultuous novel of a black man crashing through the white world's barriers of sex, color and hate.

"Magnificent" --*The New York Times*

CAPRICORNIA

Xavier Herbert

An anguished, stabbing, genuine portrait of the racial nightmare and what it means to be a proud black man in a prejudiced white society.

Capricornia is a best-seller of international fame. It is a giant, lusty novel of people divided by hate, united by passion, tormented by revenge and fear. It is the story of a primitive land, smoldering with the forbidden love between two races--the story of Norman, born of a black mother and a white father, struggling to win a place for himself.

Through the absorbing drama of one man, *Capricornia* shows the whole enormous emotional wreckage of racial hate.

"A picaresque adventure tale, a family saga, a work of social criticism. It has a Balzacian profusion of characters, all shrewdly individualized." —*Newsweek*

A535--$1.25

SAVAGE HOLIDAY

Richard Wright

This master chronicler of the black experience presents an electrifying novel of a man, a woman, and an act of violence that transcends ordinary fiction to capture the raw essence of human conflict.

A558--95¢

OTHER AWARD BOOKS
YOU'LL BE SURE TO ENJOY